Learn Bridge with Reese

First published in 1962
by Faber and Faber Limited
3 Queen Square London WC1N 3AU
Revised in 1987

Printed in Great Britain by
Richard Clay Ltd Bungay Suffolk
All rights reserved
881714
© Terence Reese 1962, 1987

795. 415
Ree
pb.

British Library Cataloguing in Publication Data

Reese, Terence
Learn bridge with Reese.
1. Contract bridge
I. Title
795.41'5   GV1282.3
ISBN 0-571-13970-1

Library of Congress Cataloging-in-Publication Data

Reese, Terence.
Learn bridge with Reese.
1. Contract-bridge. I. Title.
GV1282.3.R3439 1986   795.41'52   86-11550
ISBN 0-571-13970-1 (pbk.)

Learn Bridge with Reese

TERENCE REESE

faber and faber

LONDON · BOSTON

Foreword

Many people, I think, and not only young people, would like to play bridge if they 'knew how to start'. I hope that this book will help them, for the first three chapters are written as though for four people on a desert island who know nothing whatsoever about cards and have no one to advise them. If you can in fact watch others play while you are at this stage, that will certainly help your progress.

Bidding and play are described alternately, for the one means little without the other. Short quizzes are appended to most sections, but don't be depressed if you get some of the answers wrong. They are not merely a test of what has gone before: quite often new points of theory are introduced in this way.

Although the book is elementary throughout, I have aimed at giving an all-round picture of the game. Some books for beginners confine themselves to bidding situations which can be expressed in terms of a point count and stay clear of tricky, but important, sequences where points are no criterion. Those are the positions, in my view, where advice is most needed.

As with most games, the greatest pleasure in bridge comes from trying to improve. So when you have mastered this book and had six months' practice with better players, I hope that you will advance to one of my more learned works. Even if you only borrow it.

TERENCE REESE

Contents

9

Contents

PART THREE

First Moves in Bidding

Contents

PART FOUR

Some Stratagems in Play

PART FIVE

More about Bidding

Contents

12

PART ONE

A Description of the Game

I

If You Have Never Played Before

You know, I expect, that for a game of bridge one wants a table, four chairs and four players? And that's about all you know? Good, we will go on from there.

You are right, a pack of cards will help! Actually, it is usual and more convenient to have two packs, using them for alternate deals. Let us begin by examining the pack of fifty-two cards in relation to bridge.

The Pack

There are four suits—spades (♠), hearts (♥), diamonds (♦), clubs (♣). There are thirteen cards in each suit—Ace, King, Queen, Jack, 10, 9, 8, 7, 6, 5, 4, 3, 2. These cards are listed in order of rank—that is to say, the Ace is the highest and best card of a suit, the 2 is the lowest.

(When you take the cards out of their container you may find that one or more Jokers are included. These have no part in bridge, so remove them from the pack.)

To identify a particular card one states the rank or number and then the suit: thus, Ace of hearts, 3 of diamonds. We shall often abbreviate and use symbols: ♥ A, ♦ 3.

The top five cards of each suit—A K Q J 10—are described as honours. That is for the most part an honorary title: honour cards have no special privileges in the play, but certain combinations of honour cards in a player's hand in some circumstances earn a bonus of points.

A Description of the Game

Tricks

We have indicated already that one card may be 'higher' than another. The play at bridge consists of a series of 'tricks', to which the four players each contribute one card. The player who lays down the first card is said to lead. The others, playing in clockwise order, must, if they can, play a card of the same suit as that led. That is known as following suit. The highest card wins the trick. Imagine four players seated in the positions, North, South, East, and West, each playing a club to the following trick.

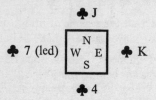

The lead was a club, East played the highest club, so he wins the trick. Having done so, he leads to the next trick.

In the next example one of the players is unable to follow suit.

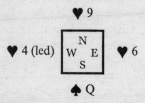

A heart was led, North played the highest heart, so he wins the trick. South, having no hearts, has discarded (the usual term when not following suit) the Queen of spades. This is a higher card than North's 9 of hearts, but is has no power to win the trick. No power, unless . . . (see next section).

The Factor of Trumps

In the play of most hands one suit has paramount rank over the others. This is the so-called 'trump suit'. Which suit, if any, is to be trumps is determined before the play begins. The importance of the trump suit is that any trump beats any card of any other suit. Clubs are trumps: you lead the Ace of spades: having no spades, I trump with the 2 of clubs. As between you and me, it is my trick.

When more than one player plays a trump, the trick is won by the highest trump. In this next example spades are trumps.

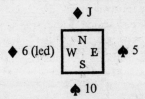

West leads the 6 of diamonds. North beats this with the Jack. East, having no diamond, trumps (an alternative word is 'ruffs') with the 5 of spades. South, who also has no diamonds, over-ruffs with the 10 of spades and wins the trick.

Now that you understand what is meant by winning a trick, you can follow this very general account of the nature of bridge:

Bridge is a partnership game in which two players sitting North and South* oppose two sitting East and West. The game consists of a series of deals in which each player has thirteen cards and each plays one card to each of thirteen tricks. The general object is to win as many tricks, and so as many points, as possible.

Of course, there is a lot more to it. We haven't touched so far on the 'bidding' that precedes the play. Bidding is half the game. But we will not anticipate. First, let us make sure, by way of question and answer, that you have not missed any points so far.

QUIZ NO. 1

(1) What are the names of the suits represented by the symbols ♠, ♥, ♦, ♣?

(2) How many cards are there of each suit?

(3) How many honours are there in each suit and how do they rank?

* These terms are just a literary convenience. At the table the opposing sides are simply 'we' and 'they'.

A Description of the Game

(4) What is meant by following suit?

(5) What is meant by discarding?

(6) After a trick has been played, who leads to the next trick?

ANSWERS TO QUIZ NO. 1

(1) Spades, hearts, diamonds, clubs.

(2) Thirteen.

(3) Five—Ace, King, Queen, Jack, 10.

(4) Playing a card of the same suit as that led.

(5) Playing a card of a different suit when unable to follow suit.

(6) The player who won the previous trick. (We have not yet studied who leads to the first trick.)

QUIZ NO. 2

In each of the following examples South is the leader. Hearts are trumps. Which player wins the trick?

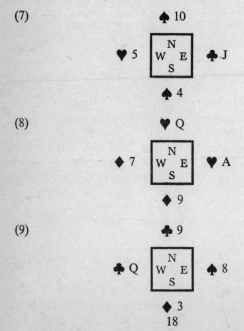

(7) ♠ 10

♥ 5   N W E S   ♣ J

♠ 4

(8) ♥ Q

♦ 7   N W E S   ♥ A

♦ 9

(9) ♣ 9

♣ Q   N W E S   ♠ 8

♦ 3

18

If You Have Never Played Before

(7) West, for he has ruffed (trumped) with the 5 of hearts.

(8) East, who has over-ruffed North's Queen of hearts with a higher trump, the Ace.

(9) South, for he led a diamond, no one has played a better diamond, and no one has ruffed.

The Bidding

You have already been advised that bidding is half the game. Bidding is a kind of auction (in fact, auction is an alternative word) in which the two sides, North-South and East-West, contest to determine whether the hand shall be played with one of the suits as trumps or with no trump suit, known as 'no-trumps'. In addition, the side that wins this auction must back itself to win a given number of tricks. It is not possible to contract to win fewer than seven tricks, the majority, and contracts are named from One, meaning seven tricks, upwards. Suppose that North and South, being partners, estimate that they can win between them ten tricks with spades as trumps. The contract is then Four Spades.

The four players speak in turn during the auction, beginning with the player who has dealt the cards and going round the table in clockwise order—South, West, North, East. Each contract that is named must, as in an ordinary auction, out-bid the previous one. A contract to win ten tricks naturally out-bids a contract to win nine. When the number of tricks is equal then precedence is decided by rank, as follows:

> No-trumps
> Spades
> Hearts
> Diamonds
> Clubs

Four Clubs overcalls Three No-Trumps, Three Hearts overcalls Three Diamonds.

The side that eventually obtains the contract has to pay a penalty if it fails to win the announced number of tricks. More-

A Description of the Game

over, it is open to the opponents, if they expect to defeat the contract, to raise the ante, borrowing a term from poker: they can 'double', which has the effect of increasing the penalty if the contract fails—also of increasing the bonus if the contract is made. Finally, a side that has been doubled can redouble, increasing penalties or bonuses still further. Doubles and redoubles do not affect the level of the contract.

We said that the players had to speak in turn during the auction, but that does not mean that each player has to make a positive bid, overcalling the previous contract. A player can always pass. In Britain this is usually expressed by the words 'No Bid'. When three players in succession have passed, the auction is over, and the last-named bid is the contract. Should all four players pass on the first round, then the hand is 'thrown in' and the deal passes to the next player.

QUIZ No. 3

(10) Who makes the first call in the auction?

(11) In what circumstances can a player redouble?

(12) What is the lowest, and what is the highest, possible contract?

ANSWERS TO QUIZ No. 3

(10) The player who dealt the cards, the dealer.

(11) Only when a bid by his side has been doubled by an opponent.

(12) One Club is the minimum, Seven No-Trumps the maximum, contract. Seven No-Trumps redoubled would be a more expensive, but not precisely a higher, contract.

QUIZ No. 4

Each of the following auctions is irregular in some respect. Where does the irregularity lie?

(13)	South	West	North	East
	1 ♦	1 ♠	1 ♥	2 ♠
	2 NT	No	3 NT	No
	No	No		

If You Have Never Played Before

(14)	South	West	North	East
	No	1 ♥	No	2 ♥
	3 ♣	No	Double	3 ♥
	No	4 ♥	No	No
	No			

(15)	South	West	North	East
	1 ♦	2 ♦	2 ♥	4 ♠
	No	No		

(16)	South	West	North	East
	1 ♣	1 ♥		4 ♥
	No	No	No	

ANSWERS TO QUIZ No. 4

(13) Since hearts rank below spades, North's One Heart was an insufficient bid. He could be called upon to amend this, but at the present stage we are not concerned with details of the Law. If East spoke without drawing attention to the insufficient bid, then it would be condoned.

(14) North has doubled his partner's bid. That comes under the heading of 'Improper Calls' and again certain Laws apply.

(15) West has bid the same suit as his opponent, but there is nothing irregular in that. All that is wrong with the auction is that North has not called over Four Spades, so that the bidding is not over. A player who thought it was over, and exposed a card, would be liable to penalty.

(16) Here East has bid out of turn. If attention were drawn to this, the bidding would revert to North, whose proper turn it was, and certain penalties would apply to East-West.

A Note on the Laws. The Laws of bridge are necessarily complicated because so many irregularities can occur and the Laws are designed to prevent a side from possibly gaining advantage from an unintentional infringement. Since a beginner reading this chapter is unlikely for some while to be playing the game for stakes of any consequence, he need not occupy his mind at this stage with study of the Laws. Irregularities in bidding and play can simply be amended without penalty.

21

A Description of the Game

Declarer and Dummy

During the bidding, as has been mentioned, all the cards are held up, but during the play (herein lies the major difference between bridge and the older game of whist) one of the hands is exposed on the table. This is the 'dummy' and dummy's cards are played throughout by his partner, the declarer. The declarer is the player who first named the denomination, a suit or no-trumps, that has become the final contract. Thus if South bids 1 NT and North raises to 3 NT, South is the declarer and North the dummy.

The opening lead is made by the player on the left of the declarer, and as soon as the lead has been made the dummy puts down his cards, sorted into suits, with the trump suit (if any) on the right. Thereafter the dummy must play a silent role. His only rights are to draw attention to an irregularity or try to prevent one from being committed. Thus he is allowed to say 'Having none?' when declarer fails to follow suit. Failure to follow suit when able to do so is called a revoke, and if the revoke is not corrected in good time there can be a serious penalty, consisting of the transfer of tricks at the end of play. Here, again, the full Law is complicated, and in a friendly game the players will adjust on a basis of equity. The other side, known as the defenders, also can warn one another against revoking.

QUIZ No. 5

After the following bidding sequences what is the contract, who is declarer, who leads, and who is dummy?

(17)	*South*	*West*	*North*	*East*
	1 ♥	1 ♠	3 ♣	3 ♠
	No	No	4 ♥	No
	No	No		

(18)	*South*	*West*	*North*	*East*
	1 ♠	2 ♣	2 NT	3 ♣
	Double	No	No	No

ANSWERS TO QUIZ NO. 5

(17) Four Hearts, played by South. West leads and North is dummy.

(18) Three Clubs doubled, played by West. North leads and East is dummy.

Part Score, Game, Slam, and Rubber

Details of the scoring are set out in the next chapter, but first we want you to be familiar with certain distinctions between contracts.

As a result of an artificial element in the scoring, contracts at a certain level have special value. They score 'game', and the first side to make two games wins the 'rubber' and a considerable bonus. At the end of a rubber scores are added up and partnerships may be changed.

The following contracts, from a love score, produce game:

> Three No-Trumps
> Four Spades or Four Hearts
> Five Diamonds or Five Clubs

Spades and hearts, in which ten tricks are sufficient for game, are known as the major suits, diamonds and clubs as the minor suits.

A successful contract for less than game produces a 'part score'. It is possible to make game in two or more steps, but as soon as game has been made by either side, a new game is begun. Part scores retain their points value but do not contribute to the next game.

A side that has won a game is said to be 'vulnerable'. From then on, both penalties for failing to make a contract (that is, penalties for undertricks) and some of the rewards for making a contract are increased. When both sides have made a game, it is 'game all' and both sides are vulnerable.

In addition to their value as game contracts, there are special rewards for bidding and making twelve tricks, a small slam, and thirteen tricks, a grand slam.

To score game or slam, a side must contract for the necessary number of tricks. A player who bids Three Hearts and makes ten tricks in the play scores only a small amount for the extra trick, called an 'overtrick'. Similarly, a player who bids Five Diamonds and makes all thirteen tricks scores game but is not credited with any bonus for slam. (That is the main difference between the modern game, Contract Bridge, and Auction Bridge, which was the standard game between 1910 and 1930).

QUIZ No. 6

What is the nature, in terms of game, slam, etc., of the following contracts:

(19) Three Spades?
(20) 3 NT?
(21) Seven Clubs?
(22) Six Hearts?
(23) Of how many games does a rubber consist?

ANSWERS TO QUIZ No. 6

(19) Part score contract.
(20) Game contract.
(21) Grand slam contract.
(22) Small slam contract.
(23) Either two or three, depending on the sequence in which the games are won. If the side that has won the first game wins the second, that ends the rubber in two games. If each side scores a game in turn, the rubber is decided by the third game.

2

The Scoring

(*A summary of scoring will be found on page* 163)

A score-sheet for bridge presents the following appearance:

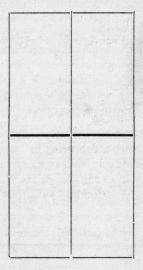

It is usual to enter the score for one's own side in the left-hand column, that of the opponents on the right. An old-fashioned score-pad may have the words 'We' and 'They' primly entered at the top of the respective columns.

All four players should keep the score. This is because the current score has a considerable effect on both bidding and play and, although indulgence would be granted to a novice, it is incorrect to draw partner's attention to the score. For example, you may have a part score, so that another part score will be sufficient for game. It is not in order to remind partner of that fact: he is supposed to be aware of it.

All the technical terms that relate to scoring have been mentioned already in Chapter 1, so now we can run through the scoring table without digression. If you have forgotten the meaning of any of the terms you can refer to the glossary at the end of the book.

Score for tricks below the line

You will have noted that the score-sheet above had a heavy line across the centre. That is because the scoring falls into two parts. Below the line is entered nothing but the score in respect of tricks bid and made. Thus, if Two Spades is bid and Three made, the score for Two Spades is written below the line, and the overtrick is recorded above (though on occasions, as we shall see below, it makes no difference if the whole score is written together).

Odd tricks (i.e. tricks beyond the number of six) in the various denominations have the following values:

> No-Trumps: first trick, 40; each subsequent trick, 30.
> Spades and hearts: each trick, 30.
> Diamonds and clubs: each trick, 20.

To score game you need 100 points below the line, and you will observe that these trick values conform to the requirements set out earlier. To make game from a love score you have to make nine tricks in no-trumps $(40 + 30 + 30)$, ten in a major (4×30) or eleven in a minor (5×20).

When either side has made a game, a line is drawn beneath it on the score-sheet, and previous part scores do not contribute to the next game. So, if you score 60 below on one hand, 40 on the next, that gives you game; but if you score 60 and then opponents make a game, you start the next game from scratch.

When a contract has been doubled, these scores below the line are doubled. When a contract has been redoubled, they are

The Scoring

multiplied by four. Thus a doubled part score contract can give you game.

Quiz No. 7

What do you score below the line for the following contracts:

(24) Three Diamonds?
(25) Four Clubs doubled?
(26) 1 NT redoubled?
(27) Six Hearts doubled?

Answers to Quiz No. 7

(24) 60.
(25) 160.
(26) 160.
(27) 360.

Quiz No. 8

(28) On successive hands the contracts made are Two Hearts by you, 3 NT by opponents, Three Clubs by you, 6 NT doubled by you, Four Diamonds, by opponents. How does the score below the line now read?

Answers to Quiz No. 8

(28) The score below the line should look like this:

60	
	100
60 380	
	80

The rubber is still unfinished.

A Description of the Game

Scores above the line

Points are scored above the line in the following ways:

1. Overtricks

Overtricks in an undoubled contract are scored at their plain trick value. Thus, Two Diamonds bid and Three made would be 40 below and 20 above. Four Hearts bid and Six made would be, strictly, 120 below and 60 above; but since game has been made in any event, it is customary to write the entire score of 180 below.

When a contract has been doubled or redoubled, overtricks have different values according to vulnerability. Not vulnerable, doubled overtricks are 100 each, redoubled overtricks 200 each. Vulnerable, they are 200 and 400 respectively.

2. Bonus for doubled and redoubled contracts

In addition to the points scored in other ways, there is a constant bonus of 50 in respect of any doubled or redoubled contract made (colloquially known as '50 for the insult').

The scoring in bridge quite soon becomes automatic, at any rate for the more common occurrences, but as it is a little complicated at first we will check as we go along.

QUIZ No. 9

How is the score entered in respect of the following contracts:
(29) Three Diamonds made with three overtricks?
(30) 2 NT made with two overtricks?
(31) Five Spades made with one overtrick?
(32) Two Clubs doubled, just made?
(33) Three Hearts doubled, vulnerable, made with two overtricks?
(34) 3 NT redoubled, not vulnerable, made with one overtrick?

ANSWERS TO QUIZ No. 9

(29) 60 below and 60 above.
(30) 70 below and 60 above.

(31) 150 below and 30 above (can be written as 180 below).

(32) Vulnerable or not, 80 below and 50 bonus above.

(33) 180 below, 450 above (200 for each overtrick and 50 bonus). Since this will be rubber there will be a bonus for that as well, but that is a separate consideration.

(34) 400 below, 250 above (200 for redoubled overtrick and 50 bonus).

3. Bonuses for small and grand slam

The bonuses for bidding and making a small slam (12 tricks) or a grand slam (13 tricks) are additional to the trick score and whatever may be scored above the line for overtricks or any other form of bonus.

Not vulnerable, small slam is 500 and grand slam 1,000.

Vulnerable, small slam is 750 and grand slam 1,500.

4. Game and rubber bonuses

No bonus points are directly entered on the score-sheet in respect of the first game by either side. The side that wins the rubber scores a bonus of 700 if the rubber has been won in two games, of 500 if the opponents have made one game.

5. Honours

For no very good reason apart from tradition, there is a bonus for holding certain honour combinations, but these honours must be held in the denomination in which the hand has been played. A player (whether declarer, dummy or a defender) who has four of the five honours in the trump suit all in his own hand scores a bonus of 100; if he has all five honours, a bonus of 150. At no-trumps a player who has four Aces scores 150.

QUIZ No. 10

What score is entered below and above the line, including rubber points, in respect of the following contracts:

(35) Six Diamonds, not vulnerable, just made?

(36) Seven Hearts, vulnerable against non-vulnerable opponents?

(37) Six Clubs doubled, at game all, made with an overtrick, declarer having four honours in clubs?

(38) 7 NT redoubled, not vulnerable, the dummy hand having four Aces?

ANSWERS TO QUIZ No. 10

(35) 120 below and 500 above.

(36) 210 below, 1,500 above for grand slam and 700 for rubber won in two games.

(37) 240 below, 750 above for small slam vulnerable, 200 for the vulnerable overtrick, 50 for doubled contract made, 500 for rubber won on the third game, 100 for four honours: in all, 1,600 above.

(38) 880 below, 1,000 above for grand slam not vulnerable, 50 for redoubled contract made, 150 for four Aces.

These mammoth scores are comparatively infrequent and a player does not need to have them in his head.

6. Penalties for undertricks

We turn now to an equally important aspect of the scoring—the penalties scored by the opposition when a side has failed to fulfil its contract. These are as follows:

(a) *Not vulnerable*
> Undoubled—50 for each undertrick.
> Doubled—100 for the first undertrick, 200 for each subsequent trick.
> Redoubled—200 for the first undertrick, 400 for each subsequent trick.

(b) *Vulnerable*
> Undoubled—100 for each undertrick.
> Doubled—200 for the first undertrick, 300 for each subsequent trick.
> Redoubled—400 for the first undertrick, 600 for each subsequent trick.

QUIZ No. 11

What penalties are scored when contracts have been defeated as follows:

(39) Two down undoubled, vulnerable?
(40) Three down doubled, not vulnerable?
(41) Two down redoubled, vulnerable?
(42) One down redoubled, not vulnerable?

ANSWERS TO QUIZ No. 11

(39) 200.
(40) 500.
(41) 1,000.
(42) 200.

7. Bonuses in an unfinished rubber

To complete the account of scoring: when a rubber cannot be completed for any reason, a side that is a game ahead scores a bonus of 300; a side that has a part score in an uncompleted game scores 50.

Settlement

At the end of a rubber scores are totalled and the difference noted. When stakes are played, it is usual to play for so much a hundred and to calculate the score to the nearest hundred. A difference of e.g. 350 counts as 3 points in Britain but as 4 in America.

3

How to Begin a Game

We have studied the elements of the game and how the scoring goes, but not so far the exact procedure from the moment that you decide to make up a game.

The Cut for Partners and Other Preliminaries

The first step, unless partnerships have been agreed in advance, is to settle who will play with whom for the first rubber. A full pack is spread across the table, face downwards. Everyone draws a card and turns it up. The players with the two highest cards are partners. They have choice of seats and also of cards, for remember that it is usual to play with two different-coloured packs. Since the deal goes to each side alternately, the side that chooses the red pack at the beginning of the rubber keeps it throughout.

The player who has cut the highest card deals the first hand. Say that he has chosen the red pack, and that he occupies the South position. He hands the cards to the opponent on his left, West, to shuffle. Having done so, West lays the pack face downward on his right. The dealer, who has the right to shuffle again if he wants to, passes the pack across to the opponent on his right, East, to cut. East divides the pack in two portions, the top half nearer the dealer. South completes the cut and begins to deal, giving the first card to the opponent on his left, the next to his partner, the third to the opponent on his right, the fourth to himself, and so on. No one should pick up his cards until the deal has been completed.

The other pack, meanwhile, which we will call the blue pack, has been shuffled by the dealer's partner. When he has finished shuffling he lays the cards down on his right.

QUIZ No. 12

(43) In the cut for partners the cards drawn are ♥ K, ♦ 4, ♣ 9, ♠ 9. Who plays with whom?

(44) Who deals the first hand?

(45) Suppose that the player in the East position is dealing: where would the other pack be?

(46) If West were dealing, to whom would he present the cards for cutting?

ANSWERS TO QUIZ No. 12

(43) The players with the King of hearts and the 9 of spades are partners, since spades rank higher than clubs.

(44) The player with the King of hearts.

(45) On his partner's right, having been shuffled.

(46) To the player on his right, South.

Bidding, Lead and Play

The deal over, all the players pick up their cards and sort them into suits. The player who dealt makes the first call—either a pass or a bid of some kind. We have already described the way in which a final contract is reached. So that you can follow the procedure more easily, we will examine a complete deal, assuming that South has distributed the cards as follows:

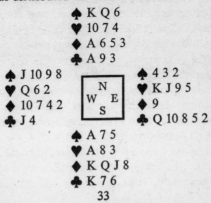

```
                    ♠ K Q 6
                    ♥ 10 7 4
                    ♦ A 6 5 3
                    ♣ A 9 3
 ♠ J 10 9 8       ┌─────────┐      ♠ 4 3 2
 ♥ Q 6 2          │    N    │      ♥ K J 9 5
 ♦ 10 7 4 2       │ W     E │      ♦ 9
 ♣ J 4            │    S    │      ♣ Q 10 8 5 2
                  └─────────┘
                    ♠ A 7 5
                    ♥ A 8 3
                    ♦ K Q J 8
                    ♣ K 7 6
```

33

A Description of the Game

This is a very flat hand on which the bidding might go:

South	West	North	East
1 NT	No	3 NT	No
No	No		

South has become the declarer, and West, the player on his left, leads the Jack of spades, detaching this card from his hand and laying it face upwards in the centre of the table. North now displays his dummy, as explained in Chapter 1. He lays the cards down in suits, but since there are no trumps there is no prescribed order of suits. You will recall that when there is a trump suit the trumps should be placed on the right.

Declarer now sees the twenty-six cards that he has to play and will pause to form a plan of campaign. The present hand is as easy as any could be, for there are three top cards in spades, one in hearts, four in diamonds, and two in clubs, making ten in all. In experienced company South might lay down his cards, claiming those ten tricks, but for the moment we will assume that he plays a trick or two before making any claim. He will detach a card from dummy, say the Queen of spades. East will play the 2 of spades and South the 5.

The trick has been won by dummy's Queen. South will gather the four cards together and lay them face downwards in front of himself. He will then lead, perhaps, the 3 of diamonds from dummy and play the King from his own hand, both opponents following suit. That will be the second trick and he will gather it and lay it aslant the first. When a trick has been turned in this way, anyone can ask to see it again until he or his partner has led or played to the succeeding trick. Thereafter no one may look at a 'quitted' trick.

Eventually, if the hand is played out until the finish, a defender will win a trick. His partner should gather it and lay it in front of himself. When the defenders win later tricks they are all placed together, so that at any time in the play anyone can see how many tricks have been won by each side.

It used to be customary for the declarer, when he had made six tricks, known as 'the book', to assemble those tricks into one pile; but that has gone out of fashion and it is better to keep the tricks separate in case there should be any cause to examine tricks at the end of play. That might happen if it were suspected that someone had revoked—failed to follow suit when able to do so.

When play is over, the result is noted and entered on everyone's score-sheet. In the present instance South will have made ten tricks—that is, Three No-Trumps with one overtrick. That will be entered as 130 below (technically 100 below and 30 above) and a line will be drawn beneath to signify that a game has been scored. Henceforth North-South will be vulnerable.

The other pack of cards, you will remember, the blue pack, has been shuffled by North and put down on his right. It is therefore at the moment on the left of West, the next dealer. West, giving the cards another shuffle if he wants to, passes this pack across to South to cut for the next deal. Meanwhile, the cards that have just been played are gathered by East, the partner of the present dealer. He shuffles (an equally common term is 'makes') them and places them on his right, ready for North to deal the hand after.

QUIZ No. 13

The contract is Four Hearts, played by West.

(47) At what point does East display his dummy?

(48) Where does East lay the heart suit?

(49) If the first trick for the defending side is won by South, where is it placed?

(50) Up to what point can a player ask to see the cards played to an earlier trick?

ANSWERS TO QUIZ No. 13

(47) After North has made the opening lead.

(48) On the right, since this is the trump suit.

(49) By convention, though there is no Law about this, it should be gathered by his partner and placed face downwards on that side of the table.

(50) Not after he or his partner has led or played to the succeeding trick.

PART TWO

First Moves in Play

4

Ways of Winning Tricks

We begin by looking at some combinations of cards in which declarer can say at once just how many tricks he can win—no more, no less.

North   (dummy)
K Q 6

A 7 5
South   (declarer)

This was the spade combination in the example hand on page 33. It is not hard to see that South can make just three tricks, the Ace, King and Queen. The only mistake he could make would be to play two of the honours on the same trick—say by leading the Ace and playing the King or Queen from dummy. It is possible to imagine a tactical situation in which that would be a clever move, but for the most part it would be very much the opposite!

North
A 9 3

K 7 6
South

This was the club distribution in the same hand. Now South can make just two tricks—the Ace and King. He cannot possibly develop an extra trick unless the opponents discard so many clubs that they have none left after two rounds have been played.

First Moves in Play

Winning Tricks with Low Cards

In the last example declarer did not hold enough cards of the suit to have any real chance of establishing an extra trick. Very often he will be able to develop tricks simply by playing out top cards and extracting—the usual word is drawing—those of the opponents. Thus, suppose that you begin by looking at this combination:

North
A 8 7 3

K Q 6 5 4
South

In top cards you hold only the Ace, King and Queen. However, you have nine cards in the two hands, and that means that there are only four against you. Unless those are all in one hand, by the time you have played off your top winners the enemy will have none left. The full distribution may be:

North
A 8 7 3

West		*East*
J 9 2		10

K Q 6 5 4
South

It is clear that if you begin by leading off the top cards you will be able to establish five winners.

Here is a combination where your chance of setting up an extra trick is not so good:

North
7 6 4

A K Q 3
South

Now you will have to be quite lucky to win a trick with the 3: here are six cards against you and you will have to find them divided 3-3 between the opposing hands. That is actually against the odds.

The greater length you hold, the fewer high cards you need to have a chance of developing tricks with low cards.

North
10 7 6 2

West   *East*
Q 9   J

A K 8 5 4 3
South

This time you hold only the Ace and King among the top honours, but you have ten cards between the two hands and will make all six tricks unless the three outstanding cards are all in the same hand.

With a little experience calculations of this sort become automatic and instantaneous. It may seem strange advice, but when you answer the quizzes in this chapter we suggest that you attempt a snap answer, even if it be the wrong one, rather than be laboriously certain that you have it right. The sooner you can acquire a sense of distribution, assessing at a glance how many tricks you may make in each suit, the more quickly you will be in a position to plan the play of a complete hand.

QUIZ No. 14

With the combinations below:

(*a*) How many tricks can South be sure of winning however the cards are distributed against him?

(*b*) How many tricks can he win if the distribution is as favourable as it can be?

(51)   A Q 6 2   (52)   A Q 5 4
        K 8 7 4   K J

(53)   J 7 6   (54)   A Q 6 4 3
      A K Q 4 2   K 10

(55)   K 8 7 3
     A Q 9 5 4 2

41

First Moves in Play

(51) (*a*) Three, if the distribution is 4-1 or 5-0.
    (*b*) Four, if the adverse distribution is 3-2.

(52) (*a*) Four, by leading out the King and Jack, then crossing to the North hand in another suit to make the Ace and Queen.
    (*b*) Four.

(53) (*a*) Only four, if the distribution is unluckily 5-0.
    (*b*) Five.

(54) (*a*) Only three are certain.
    (*b*) Five, if the distribution is 3-3.

(55) (*a*) Six, for there are only three cards outstanding and these must fall under the Ace, King and Queen.
    (*b*) Six.

Winning Tricks by Promotion

Apart from laying down Aces, Kings, and Queens, declarer can establish secondary tricks, as it were, by forcing out enemy high cards. This is a simple example:

QJ6

10 7 5   A 8 4 2

K 9 3

South has no immediate trick to 'cash' (this term is often used instead of 'make') but he can establish two certain winners by forcing out East's Ace. He can begin by leading the Queen from dummy; if East does not capture the trick another round is led.

K J 5 3 2

A 9 4   10 8 7

Q 6

Owing to the favourable distribution South is able to make four tricks with this combination.

In the next example South plans to force out two adverse winners:

Q J 9 4

A 8 5   K 3 2

10 7 6

South forces out the Ace and King in turn. Given time, he will make the remaining two tricks.

Establishing Tricks for Low Cards

Another way to arrive at extra tricks is by conceding a trick on a later round in order to promote low cards as winners.

A Q 6 4 3

J 9 5 2   8 7

K 10

The North-South cards are the same as in Question 54. We noted then that only three tricks were certain and that five were possible. A very common result would be to end up with four. After the Ace, King, and Queen have been played off, West is left with the Jack, which by that time will be master. The fourth round is conceded to the Jack, and then the fifth round will be won by North.

A 8 7 4 2

K 9 3

This is a very common holding. South must concede at least one trick, for there are five cards against him, including the Queen, Jack, and 10, and these five cards cannot all be eliminated in two rounds; but so long as the distribution is 3-2 one trick can be conceded and four will be won.

K 5

J 9 6   A 10 8

Q 7 4 3 2

This time declarer promotes tricks in two ways: he drives out two adverse winners and makes two 'long' cards, as they are called, by taking advantage of the 3-3 break. The first lead is the

2 towards the King. This is taken by the Ace. When South is next in the lead he plays off the Queen and another. West wins this third round with the Jack, but the remaining cards in the South hand have been promoted.

QUIZ No. 15

Assuming that he has time to force out enemy high cards and regain the lead,

(*a*) How many tricks can South be sure of establishing with the combinations below?

(*b*) How many tricks can he win if the distribution is favourable?

(56) Q 7 5 3
       K J 4

(57) Q 10 6 4 2
       J 5 3

(58)   10 9 4
      J 8 7 6 3 2

(59) A 9 5 3
      8 7 6 4 2

(60) A 8 6 5 3
      J 4

ANSWERS TO QUIZ No. 15

(56) (*a*) Two.
    (*b*) Three, if the distribution is 3-3. (There is actually another chance: by leading twice up to K J 4 declarer can win three tricks when East has the Ace only once guarded.)

(57) (*a*) Only one, at the worst, one defender holding A K 9 8 7.
    (*b*) Three, if the cards are divided 3-2.

(58) (*a*) Three.
    (*b*) Four, if the cards are divided 2-2.

(59) (*a*) Two—the Ace and, at worst, the fifth round.
    (*b*) Four, if the cards are divided 2-2.

(60) (*a*) Only one, if an opponent holds as many as five.
    (*b*) Three, if the distribution is 3-3.

5

Going from Hand to Hand

In this chapter we advance to the play of two hands in combination. If you find it difficult, as some do, to follow a hand on paper, you can lay out actual cards. Still, that will slow you down somewhat, and on the whole we recommend that you practise forming a mental picture. A good method is to write down the hands as shown and tick off the cards as they are played.

Considerations of Entry

One of the suit combinations presented in the last chapter was the following:

	North	
	A 8 7 3	
West		*East*
J 9 2		10
	K Q 6 5 4	
	South	

We commented that by leading off the top cards you could establish five winners. That is true, but a small problem arises that might trip you up in the play of an actual hand. Suppose that you play the King from South and the 3 from North: then the 4 and the Ace, followed by the 7 and the Queen. That will leave the 8 alone in North, while South has the 6 5. Now the run of the suit has been obstructed. That will not matter if there is a quick and convenient entry back to South, but if no such entry is available a trick will have been thrown away. South has quite a simple solution in the present case: he must take care to 'unblock', as it is called, by playing the 7, 8, and Ace from North on the first three rounds, keeping the 3 to play on the 6.

Such small problems occur all the time in bridge. On this first hand South has simply to play his top cards in the right order.

♠ A K
♥ A 6 4 2
♦ 9 6 4
♣ 7 6 5 3

♦ K led

♠ Q J 5 3
♥ K Q
♦ A 5 2
♣ A 10 8 4

The contract is 3 NT, played by South, and West leads the King of diamonds. The first step is to count the certain winners to see how close you are to the nine tricks you need. Here there are four top tricks in spades, three in hearts, one in diamonds and one in clubs. You have just to be careful that you cash your winners in the right order. For example, it would be a mistake to win with the Ace of diamonds and straight away play off dummy's Ace and King of spades. To be sure of three tricks in hearts you must play off the King and Queen before using the two entries to dummy. So, the correct sequence is: Ace of diamonds, King and Queen of hearts; a spade to the Ace; King of spades and, while you are in dummy, Ace of hearts; then back to Ace of clubs to make the Queen and Jack of spades.

In the next example South has to force out an enemy high card and must again take care not to land himself in the wrong hand at the wrong time.

♠ 5 3 2
♥ J 4
♦ Q J 9 6 2
♣ A 6 5

Going from Hand to Hand

♠ 7 led

♠ A Q 4
♥ A K 6 2
♦ K 5 4
♣ J 9 2

Again South plays in 3 NT and this time the 7 of spades is led. A low card is played from North and East puts on the King. Now it is by no means always right to capture tricks at the first opportunity, but on this hand there is a sound tactical reason why South should take the first spade: if he does not, then opponents, seeing the long diamond suit in dummy, may switch to clubs. If the Ace of clubs is forced out before South has established tricks in diamonds he may find himself cut off from dummy's good suit.

South wins the first trick with ♠ A, therefore, noting that he will be home if he can make two spades, two hearts, four diamonds and one club. At once he sets about establishing the diamonds. The first play should in fact be a low diamond, not the King. This is because West might have the Ace alone: if he were able to top the King with the Ace, then a trick would be established for East's 10 8 7 3.

We will suppose, however, that on the lead of the 4 of diamonds West plays the 3, North the Jack and East the 7. It is apparent that one of the opponents has held up the Ace; that is common play in a situation of this kind where declarer is playing to establish a long suit. In dummy with ♦ J South persists with the diamonds, returning the 2. Suppose that East now plays the Ace: South must be careful to unblock by playing the King. If he omitted to do that, and the opponents attacked dummy's entry, the Ace of clubs, then South's King of diamonds would block the run of the suit. So long as West also follows to this round of diamonds the rest of the suit will be good and South will make a minimum of nine tricks as planned.

Drawing Trumps

Next we look at the play in a trump contract. In the first example South has arrived at a small slam, Six Spades.

47

First Moves in Play

♠ K 6 4
♥ A Q J 5 2
♦ 4 2
♣ A 4 3

♦ 3 led

♠ A Q J 7 5
♥ K
♦ A 10 8 5
♣ Q 6 2

West leads the 3 of diamonds, East plays the Queen, and South, having no reason to hold up, the Ace. Now, unless the spades are particularly unkind, breaking 5-0, declarer will make five tricks in that department and lose none. What of the hearts? Here there is a certainty of four tricks and a fair chance of five, this depending on a 4-3 break. At first sight, therefore, there is a prospect of ten tricks in the major suits plus the two minor suit Aces. If the hearts provide only four tricks, the twelfth may come from the Queen of clubs. That will depend on the position of the club King, which we will examine in a moment.

Suit contracts have to be approached somewhat differently from no-trump contracts. Always the first question is, shall I draw trumps? There are many exceptions, as we shall see in a later chapter, but a fairly safe proposition is that unless you can see a good reason not to draw trumps, you should do so.

After winning with ♦ A, therefore, you lay down Ace of spades, West playing the 3 and East the 9. You follow with a low spade to the King, on which East discards a club. No matter, there are only two spades left; you draw those, discarding a diamond from dummy on the fourth round. Next you cash the King of hearts, then enter dummy with the Ace of clubs.

While you were playing off the spades you were keeping an eye on East's discards, especially to see if he threw a heart. In fact, he did not. All follow to the Ace of hearts, but when you play the Queen of hearts, West discards a diamond.

Now you may have to count the hearts to determine whether or not the last two are good. Better than counting is to acquire a

48

sense of distribution: West having turned up with a doubleton (two cards), the distribution round the table must be 5-5-2-1. After you have cashed the Jack, the following cards are left:

♠ —
♥ 5
♦ —
♣ 4 3

♠ 7
♥ —
♦ —
♣ Q 6

The lead is in dummy and you play a club towards the Queen. If East plays the King and leads a diamond you can ruff with your last trump and make the Queen of clubs.

The next hand is played in a game contract, Four Hearts.

♠ Q 7 4 2
♥ J 6 3
♦ 7 5 2
♣ A 8 6

♦ Q led

♠ K J 10
♥ A K 8 7 5 2
♦ 4
♣ K 5 2

The defenders win the first trick in diamonds and we will say that they switch to clubs at trick 2. That is actually better play on their part than continuing diamonds. Since he has ample entries to his own hand, South takes this trick with the King of clubs and leads out the Ace of hearts. The Queen does not drop, but both opponents follow suit. Declarer then lays down the King of hearts, and this time West discards a diamond.

The opponents have the master trump now, the Queen, but declarer can afford to leave that at large. It would be a mistake to play another heart, for then the defence might continue clubs, establishing a trick in that suit before the Ace of spades had been knocked out.

Instead of playing a third trump South leads the King of spades and, if that is not taken, continues with the Jack. Best for the defence now is to win with ♠ A and play another club, forcing out the Ace. This is now the position:

> ♠ Q 7
> ♥ J
> ♦ 7 5
> ♣ 8
>
> ♠ 10
> ♥ 8 7 5 2
> ♦ —
> ♣ 5

South has lost two tricks and the Queen of hearts is still out against him. He would like to return to ♠ 10 and then cross to dummy for a discard of a club on ♠ Q, but dummy has no entry. The only hope, therefore, is to play off the Queen of spades: if the suit was originally divided 3-3 the 7 will be good.

If the defenders had continued diamonds at trick 2, the play would have been easier. South would ruff, play off ♥ A K and then set about the spades. With the clubs twice held, he would have plenty of time to establish a discard on the Queen of spades.

6

The Factor of Position

You may remember that one of the contracts in the last chapter depended, or might have depended, on finding the King of clubs favourably placed. Declarer had A 4 3 in dummy, Q 6 2 in his own hand: to make a trick with the Queen he had to find the King on his right, in front of the Queen. He had, moreover, to lead up to the Queen, not away from it. There you have one of the fundamental principles of the game—that for the most part it pays to lead towards honours and not away from them. The simplest example is the lead towards an unsupported King.

K 5

A 4   Q J

7 2

It is apparent that so long as he does not have to lead from his own hand North will make a trick with the King.

K Q 5

A J 8   10 9 7 2

6 4 3

Now two tricks can be won by leading twice towards the K Q. If the lead comes from North, on the other hand, the King or Queen will be headed by West's Ace and only one trick will be made by declarer.

Simple Finesse

If we change the cards around a little we arrive at one of the commonest manœuvres in the game—the finesse.

51

First Moves in Play

A Q

K 4   10 3

6 5

South leads the 6, West plays the 4 and declarer puts in the Queen from dummy. Because of the favourable position of the King, the Queen holds: the finesse has won.

Q J 10 4

8   K 6 3

A 9 7 5 2

This is another example of a simple finesse against the King. The Queen is led from North, East plays low, and so does South. When the Queen holds, the Jack is led from dummy and South finesses again. On the next round the King is captured by the Ace, and South makes all five tricks.

6 4

9 3   Q 8 7 5

A K J 10 2

This time declarer finesses twice against the Queen. On the first round he leads the 4 from dummy and finesses the Jack. When next in dummy he leads the 6 and finesses the 10, so making all five tricks.

In the next two examples the finesse is played from a less powerful combination:

K J 9 4

Q 7 6 3   A 5

10 8 2

South leads the 10 or 8 and West plays low. Declarer plays low from dummy, and we will say that East puts on the Ace. When South regains the lead he takes another finesse against the Queen and ends up by making three tricks.

K 7

A 9 5   J 6 3

Q 10 8 4 2

52

This time the finesse is taken against the Jack. South begins by leading the 2 towards dummy's K 7. Generally speaking, it is not good play for a defender to put up a high card when second to play, for the best use of high cards is to kill other high cards. West plays the 5, therefore, and declarer goes up with the King, which holds the trick. The 7 is returned from dummy and East plays the 6. Now South has the choice of going up with the Queen or finessing the 10. The finesse is likely to be the better play, for if East had had the Ace he would probably have used it to kill the King. The finesse of the 10 is successful as the cards lie and with the aid of the favourable division South can make four tricks.

Double and Combination Finesses

In the examples so far the declarer has been taking a finesse against a single card. Often he will have to attack a suit in which he hopes to find at any rate one out of two cards favourably placed. This is a 'combination finesse':

<pre>
              A J 10
      Q 7 3   K 8 4 2
              9 6 5
</pre>

South begins by leading a low card and finessing the 10. He is not especially hopeful about this, and as expected East wins the trick. On the next round, however, a finesse of the Jack is successful.

This is another holding that presents a combination finesse:

<pre>
              K 10 9 4
      Q 6 3   A J 5
              8 7 2
</pre>

South leads the 8, plays low from dummy, and loses to the Jack. On the next round he finesses again, and this time the 9 fetches the Ace. Thus two tricks are won by each side.

Declarer is said to play a double finesse when he plays for two cards to be right. This is the standard example:

A Q 10 5

6 4 2

South leads the 2 and puts on the 10 from dummy. If this loses
to the Jack, a later finesse of the Queen can be taken. South will do
best when West holds both King and Jack. In that case the 10 will
win and South will return to hand for a later finesse of the Queen.

Quiz No. 16

Assuming that he has ample entries to both hands, how should
declarer play the following combinations, and how many tricks
can he win if the distribution is favourable?

(61) A 10 9 5 4
   J 7 3

(62) K J 4
  7 6 5 2

(63) A Q 7 5 3
  J 6 4 2

(64) J 7 4 2
  A 10 6 3

(65) Q 9 5 3
  J 6 4

Answers to Quiz No. 16

(61) This is a combination finesse in which South plays for the
missing honours to be divided (or both in West's hand). He begins
by leading the 3 and finessing the 9 unless West plays an honour.
If the 9 loses to the King or Queen he finesses later against the
outstanding honour. He has a good chance of making four tricks.

(62) Here South can take a double finesse against the A Q. On
the first round he leads towards the Jack. If he is lucky enough to
find West with precisely Ace, Queen and one other card, he will
make three tricks eventually.

(63) South leads low and puts in the Queen from dummy,
making five tricks if West has King and one other card or King
single. Note that it would be a mistake to lead the Jack, for then
if West had the singleton King and East 10 9 8, the 10 would win
the third round. In general, a low card should be led for a finesse
unless declarer has a strong sequence such as Q J 10 9 or J 10 9 8.

54

The Factor of Position

(64) The best play is to lead low from North and put in the 10, laying down the Ace on the next round. That wins three tricks when East has K Q x or K x or Q x (x standing for any low card).

(65) With this combination South can finesse against the 10. First he leads low from North and we will say that the Jack is headed by the King or Ace. On the next round the best chance is to finesse the 9. South will make two tricks in the suit if West has K 10 x or A 10 x, and there are other possibilities as well.

When a Finesse may not be Correct Play

Some positions are a little deceptive: they seem to present the opportunity for a finesse, whereas in fact a finesse, if playable at all, can scarcely gain. Take the combination mentioned at the beginning of this chapter:

A 4 3

Q 6 2

You may wonder why you should not lead the Queen and run it. The answer is that if West has the King he will play it on the Queen, and all you will make is the Ace. The way to take advantage of a favourable lie is to play towards the Queen: you will win two tricks if East has the King.

With the following combination a finesse is playable but is not the best way to win the maximum number of tricks:

A 4 3

Q J 7 2

If two tricks are all you want and you cannot afford to lose a trick, then you must lead the Queen and finesse if West plays low. But suppose you want to make three tricks: then your best chance is to lead up to the two honours. The distribution may be:

(i)	A 4 3		(ii)	A 4 3	
10 8		K 9 6 5		10 8 6 5	K 9
	Q J 7 2			Q J 7 2	

A little experiment will show that in both cases leading the Queen actually costs a trick as compared with playing towards the Q J 7 2.

The essential factor in these examples is that even if you find the adverse high card in a position where it can be captured your intermediate cards are such that you cannot benefit. Compare these two holdings:

(iii)   A K 10 6   (iv)   A K 5 4

        J 9 3   J 6 3

In the first example you can lead the Jack and finesse, for if West covers the Jack with the Queen you will make all the tricks. In example (iv), where you are missing the 10 and 9 as well as the Queen, the finesse cannot gain. Your best chance for three tricks, actually, is to play the Ace and then low from North towards the J 6: that will establish a trick for the Jack whenever East has the Queen, and you will also make three tricks when the distribution is 3-3. If you needed three quick tricks however, and could not afford to lose the lead, you would have to lead out the Ace and King, hoping to drop the Queen in two rounds.

There will often be a choice between taking a finesse and playing for an honour to drop.

(v)   K J 7 6 2   (vi)   K J 7 6 4 2

      A 8 5   A 8 5

In both cases you begin by laying down the Ace and then lead up to the K J combination. Suppose that West follows suit and that the Queen has not appeared: you have to choose between finessing the Jack and playing the King, hoping to drop the Queen. In example (v), where you have only eight cards in the two hands, the finesse is the better chance mathematically. In example (vi), where you can see nine cards, the odds just favour playing for the drop, but there is not a lot in it and in actual play there may be indications that a 3-1 break is more likely than 2-2.

The Factor of Position

How should declarer play the following combinations to make the maximum number of tricks?

(66) K Q 10 3
     A 7 2

(67) A 10 8 4
     K J 9 3

(68)   J 5 4
     A Q 7 3 2

(69)   J 7 5 3
     A Q 8 6 4 2

(70)   Q 7 3
     K 8 6 4 2

ANSWERS TO QUIZ No. 17

(66) South should begin with a low card to the King, return the 3 to the Ace, and lead the 7. A problem arises only if both opponents follow suit throughout and the Jack is still missing after West has played. West may have J x x x and East x x, or West x x x and East J x x. Other things being equal, the odds slightly favour playing for the drop rather than finessing the 10.

(67) Declarer has what is known as a 'two-way' finesse: he can play either defender for the Queen. Psychologically, a good move is to lead the Jack, for West may give away the position of the Queen by covering. If West plays low, put on the Ace and finesse on the way back.

(68) Declarer's only chance to make all five tricks against best defence is to lead a low card from dummy and finesse the Queen, playing East for K x. Note that it would be a mistake to lead the Jack, for then East, with K x, would cover and West would control the third round.

(69) With ten cards, missing the King, the finesse is a better proposition than playing for a singleton King to drop from West.

(70) No finesse is playable in the ordinary sense, but South has a chance to win four tricks when an opponent has the Ace only once guarded. Say that South begins by leading the 2 to the Queen, and this holds. On the way back he should play low from hand, hoping that West will have to play the Ace, beating the air. It is equally possible to play East for A x; in that case the first lead will be from North up to the King.

PART THREE

First Moves in Bidding

7

No-Trump Bidding

In this chapter we shall study hands on which the bidding may be opened with calls of One, Two or Three No-Trumps. This is one of the easiest departments of bidding because to a large extent it can be reduced to a formula of 'points'. There is an almost universal system of valuation for high cards, as follows:

Ace	equals	4 points
King	,,	3 points
Queen	,,	2 points
Jack	,,	1 point

You will appreciate that it is easier to say that a hand has 16 points than to say that it contains two Aces, one King, two Queens and one Jack. Therein lies the usefulness of the point count: it is a convenient way of expressing the value of a hand in terms of high cards.

Opening 1 NT

Among bridge players in general there are many different theories about the strength demanded for an opening 1 NT. An average hand contains 10 points and some players open 1 NT with about a King above average. That is described as a 'weak' no-trump. Many players make a distinction between vulnerable and non-vulnerable openings. We are going to suggest a fairly strong no-trump at any score—namely 16 to 18 points.

Apart from this requirement in high cards, the hand should be reasonably balanced. When you play in no-trumps you cannot arrest the run of a long enemy suit in which you have no guard, so on hands containing a singleton or worthless doubleton it is better to begin with a suit call rather than suggest that you have all-round protection. The distributions most suitable for a no-trump opening are 4-3-3-3, 4-4-3-2, and 5-3-3-2.

QUIZ No. 18

   (*a*) What is the point-count value of the following hands?
   (*b*) Are they suitable for an opening 1 NT?
   (71) ♠ Q 7 3 ♥ K Q 8 ♦ A J 4 ♣ Q 10 7 6
   (72) ♠ A K 5 ♥ K 7 ♦ Q J 9 3 ♣ K J 8 5
   (73) ♠ K Q 10 5 4 ♥ 7 3 ♦ A J ♣ A Q 4 2
   (74) ♠ K 10 ♥ A J 8 ♦ K Q J 9 6 ♣ J 10 8
   (75) ♠ A Q 8 ♥ K Q 6 2 ♦ K 7 4 ♣ K Q 3

ANSWERS TO QUIZ No. 18

   (71) (*a*) 14.
      (*b*) The distribution is suitable and the honours well divided over all the suits, but the hand is 2 points short of the standard requirement.
   (72) (*a*) 17.
      (*b*) This hand is suitable for 1 NT in terms of both strength and character.
   (73) (*a*) 16.
      (*b*) The strength is right, but the distribution 5-4-2-2 is somewhat unbalanced and a further objection is that the holding in hearts is weak. It is better to open One Spade; a contract in no-trumps may still be reached.
   (74) (*a*) 15.
      (*b*) The hand is superficially one point short, but there is a useful five-card minor and what are known as 'good intermediates'—that is, a leavening of 10's and 9's that can play an important role in no-trump contracts. By all means open 1 NT and do not be too rigid in applying the point-count test.

(75) (*a*) 19.

    (*b*) This time you are a point 'over' but it is a flat sort of hand with no intermediates. Again open 1 NT, establishing that the point-count is your servant, not your master.

Raises of 1 NT

The partner of the opening bidder is called the 'responder' and when he gives direct support to his partner's declaration he is said to 'raise'.

Three No-Trumps, as you know, is a game contract and therefore an important objective. If you cannot make game, or are not going to bid game, there is no advantage in playing in 2 NT rather than 1 NT. Scoring 70 below the line instead of 40 means little, but it is bad to go one down instead of making 1 NT.

Responder's first thought, therefore, except on strong hands where he can look for a slam, is whether there is a prospect of game in a suit or no-trumps. If his hand is of no-trump type, containing no singleton, he need not look for any other denomination.

There are exactly 40 points in the pack and a side that has 25, with no pronounced weakness, will normally have a sound play for 3 NT. On that basis, raises are easy to calculate. When partner opens 1 NT you expect him to have 16 to 18 points. If you have no more than 6 points then game must be doubtful and you should pass. With 7 or 8 you raise to 2 NT, inviting him to bid game if not minimum. With 9 points you raise to 3 NT.

QUIZ No. 19

Partner has opened 1 NT. How should you respond on the following hands?

(76) ♠ Q 4 3 ♥ A 10 7 4 2 ♦ Q 7 6 ♣ 5 3

(77) ♠ Q 10 5 2 ♥ J 7 ♦ K Q 8 6 4 ♣ 10 6

(78) ♠ J 5 2 ♥ J 4 ♦ 9 7 3 2 ♣ A K 10 6

(79) ♠ 8 7 3 ♥ 7 6 4 2 ♦ J 4 2 ♣ A Q 3

(80) ♠ A Q 8 ♥ K J 9 4 ♦ A 8 7 2 ♣ 10 6

ANSWERS TO QUIZ NO. 19

(76) Here you have 8 points and a fair five-card suit. You have a sound raise to 2 NT, and 3 NT would not be a mistake.

(77) Again you have 8 points, but this time you have two 10's and your five-card suit has two high honours, so that it should not require any establishment. You should raise to 3 NT.

(78) Not a wonderful hand, but the 9 points, with honours in three suits, justify a raise to game.

(79) This time you have a very flat 7 points and it is a disadvantage that so much of your strength is in one suit. Game will be uphill work at best, so we recommend a pass.

(80) Here you have 14 points, giving an average expectancy of about 31 in the two hands. That is not enough for slam on balanced hands, so you raise to 3 NT simply. To play in 6 NT, when you have no long suit, you want upwards of 33 points.

Suit Responses to 1 NT

When your hand contains a singleton or void (none of a suit) it will generally be better to suggest a suit contract. A simple take-out into Two of a suit is not a strong call: it says only that you see a better chance of making eight tricks in the suit than of making 1 NT. With stronger hands you jump to Three of a suit. That is a forcing response: even when he has a minimum the no-trump bidder must keep the bidding open either by raising the suit or by bidding 3 NT.

With very bad hands—less than 4 points—it is advisable to pass 1 NT even when unbalanced. With 5 to 7 points you take out into your long suit. With 8 points and a good major suit you can generally invite game. When your long suit is a minor it may be in order to raise to game in no-trumps rather than aspire to make eleven tricks in the suit.

No-Trump Bidding

Partner has opened 1 NT. How should you respond on the following hands?

(81) ♠ J 7 6 4 2   ♥ 5 2   ♦ K 9 6 3   ♣ 8 4

(82) ♠ Q 8 5 3   ♥ —   ♦ K 10 7 6 2   ♣ 9 4 3 2

(83) ♠ Q 10 8 6 4   ♥ A 8 3   ♦ 4   ♣ K 9 7 2

(84) ♠ 7   ♥ Q 8 4   ♦ 7 3 2   ♣ A Q 10 7 6 3

(85) ♠ A 4   ♥ K Q 7 5 3   ♦ A Q 9 5   ♣ 7 4

ANSWERS TO QUIZ No. 20

(81) Do not disturb 1 NT. Apart from the fact that you are weak, you are as likely to make 1 NT as Two Spades.

(82) Respond Two Diamonds.

(83) With 9 points and a fair major suit you force with Three Spades. If partner's rebid is 3 NT you should let him play that.

(84) If this six-card suit were a major you would suggest game in the suit. However, you are not so likely to make Five Clubs. It would not be a mistake to bid Three Clubs, but just as good is to jump to 3 NT, for that is where your best chance of game lies. Partner should have at least one guard in spades and your clubs are sure to develop several tricks.

(85) Now you have 15 points made up of top cards and a slam is likely. For the moment it is sufficient to jump to Three Hearts. Remember that the jump is forcing and that partner is obliged to respond.

Opening Bids of 2 NT and Responses

To open 2 NT you require to be about an Ace stronger than for 1 NT. The usual standard is 21-22 points, but as always you can take long suits and good intermediates into the reckoning. Possession of a five-card suit is no bar to a 2 NT opening. You should normally have at least a Queen, or four low cards, in every suit.

First Moves in Bidding

With a hand suitable for play in no-trumps, responder can raise to 3 NT on 4 points. Any suit response at the level of Three is forcing, though it does not necessarily show a strong hand.

Quiz No. 21

Are the following hands suitable for an opening bid of 2 NT?

(86) ♠ A J 8   ♥ K Q 8 6   ♦ A 9 4   ♣ A J 3

(87) ♠ K 5   ♥ Q 3 2   ♦ A K Q 10 7   ♣ A Q 2

(88) ♠ A Q J   ♥ A Q 4   ♦ 8 4   ♣ A K J 3 2

(89) ♠ A 4   ♥ A K J   ♦ K Q J 4   ♣ K Q 3 2

Answers to Quiz No. 21

(86) This 19-point hand is a little strong for 1 NT, not strong enough for 2 NT. Such hands are expressed by opening with One of a suit and rebidding 3 NT over a minimum response.

(87) The almost solid five-card minor suit makes this 20-point hand a good 2 NT opening.

(88) This hand falls within the appropriate range of points, but the diamonds are unprotected, the long suit may require support, and there are values in both the majors, suggesting that game may be safer in one of those. It is better to approach with One Club.

(89) This hand contains 23 points but in proportion to its high cards is not especially powerful. There is nothing wrong with 2 NT.

Quiz No. 22

Partner has opened 2 NT. How should you respond on the following hands?

(90) ♠ J 7 4   ♥ 6 2   ♦ A 9 7 3 2   ♣ 7 5 4

(91) ♠ 10 7 5 3 2   ♥ 4   ♦ J 8 6 2   ♣ J 7 4

(92) ♠ 6   ♥ K J 8 7 5   ♦ Q J 6 2   ♣ 6 4 3

Answers to Quiz No. 22

(90) Respond 3 NT. There is no point in bidding Three Dia-

monds, for you do not propose to play for game in the suit. If partner were to raise you in diamonds, you would be sorry you had by-passed 3 NT.

(91) It is possible that the hand would be safer in Three Spades than 2 NT, but remember that partner will not pass Three Spades. You should let him play in 2 NT.

(92) Bid Three Hearts, allowing partner to choose between Four Hearts and 3 NT.

Opening Bids of 3 NT

In a later chapter we shall describe a conventional way of bidding very strong hands. When that convention is played, 3 NT is an infrequent opening, generally based on a long and solid minor suit with some protection in at least two other suits, something like:

♠ 4 2   ♥ A Q   ♦ K 10   ♣ A K Q 8 7 5 3

When no such convention is played, 3 NT suggests about 23 to 25 points and balanced distribution.

Stayman Convention

So as not to distract, we did not mention the popular Stayman Convention when discussing responses to 1 NT. When this convention is played a response of Two Clubs to 1 NT asks the opener to name a major suit in which he holds four cards. Lacking a four-card major, the opener rebids Two Diamonds.

8

Opening Suit
Bids of One and Responses

To open the bidding with One of a suit you require about 13 points when you have no long suit. This can be reduced to 12 points when you have a five-card suit, and to 11 points when you have a good six-card suit or two five-card suits. These are some examples:

(i)   ♠ K 10 7   ♥ Q 6 4 2   ♦ A 5   ♣ K J 8 3

(ii) ♠ A Q 10 9 7 3   ♥ 4   ♦ A J 7   ♣ 10 3 2

(iii) ♠ 4 3   ♥ K Q 10 6 4   ♦ A 5 4 2   ♣ Q 7

Hand (i) has 13 points; open One Club. Hand (ii) has only 11 points in high cards but you can add 2 points for the good six-card suit and open One Spade. Hand (iii) has 11 points and a five-card suit, for which you can add 1 point. You might open this if you were third in hand after two passes, but it is under strength for One Heart in any other position.

When there is a Choice of Suits

There are no strict rules as to what constitutes a biddable suit, but it is preferable to avoid opening a four-card major that is weaker than K J x x.

When you have more than one biddable suit this is how you decide between them:

1. *When the suits are of unequal length, bid the longer suit first.*

2. *When you have two five-card suits bid the higher-ranking first.*

3. *When you have only four-card suits bid the suit that is imme-diately below your short suit—your singleton or doubleton.*

This last rule applies especially to moderate hands where it is desirable to keep the bidding low.

Quiz No. 23

As dealer, what do you bid on the following hands?

(93) ♠ K 10 8 6 4   ♥ A Q J 5 2   ♦ J 4   ♣ 3

(94) ♠ A Q 9 5   ♥ 6   ♦ K J 8 7 6   ♣ Q 6 3

(95) ♠ 4   ♥ A J 8 6 4   ♦ K   ♣ Q 8 7 6 4 2

Answers to Quiz No. 23

(93) One Spade. You have 11 points in high cards and count 1 for each of the five-card suits. As between the two biddable suits, you open the higher-ranking. Do not be influenced by the fact that the hearts are stronger.

(94) One Diamond, bidding the longer suit first.

(95) No Bid. The suits are not robust and you cannot attach the same value to the singleton King of diamonds as if it were part of a longer suit.

Quiz No. 24

The following hands contain only four-card suits. On these the general rule, as we said above, is to open the suit below the single-ton or doubleton. The reason for that is to keep the bidding low, should partner respond in the weak suit. When that consideration does not seem important, then it may well be right to open the higher suit.

As dealer, what do you bid on the following?

(96) ♠ A Q 10 4   ♥ 6 5   ♦ K 7 6   ♣ A 8 4 2

(97) ♠ 6 5   ♥ A Q 7 3   ♦ A 10 7   ♣ K Q 6 3

(98) ♠ K 8 7   ♥ Q 7 4 2   ♦ K Q 5   ♣ A 7 3

First Moves in Bidding

(99) ♠ Q 10 7 3   ♥ A J 6 2   ♦ A K 6 4   ♣ 5

(100) ♠ A K 10 4   ♥ 6 3   ♦ Q 9 8 2   ♣ A K 4

ANSWERS TO QUIZ NO. 24

(96) One Club. If partner responds in your weak suit, hearts, the bidding will still be at a low level.

(97) One Heart, the suit below your doubleton; but One Club would not be a mistake.

(98) One Club. With only 14 points and no intermediates you are not strong enough for 1 NT. To bid a major suit as weak as Q x x x is undesirable, especially on a hand that has no other suit. The solution is to bid a three-card minor.

(99) One Heart. When the singleton is in clubs the suit-below-the-singleton is technically spades; but when the spades are as weak as this it is sounder to open One Heart.

(100) One Spade. Do not lose sight of the fact that the reason for the suit-below-the-short-suit rule is to keep the bidding at a safe level on minimum hands. It would not be a bad mistake to open One Diamond here, but One Spade is tactically better. There is no reason to fear a response of Two Hearts from partner, for the opening hand is better than minimum and can rebid 2 NT.

Responding to Bids of One

We will assume for the moment that partner's opening bid has not been overcalled by the next player. Responses can then be divided into four main groups:

A. Weak bids that show limited strength.
B. Changes of suit that may be quite weak or quite strong.
C. Encouraging bids, just short of game.
D. Strong bids, forcing at least to game.

A. Weak bids that show limited strength

There are two bids that say to partner: 'I have just a little for you: don't bid again unless you are quite strong.'

These two bids are 1 NT, showing a balanced hand with about

6 to 9 points, and a single raise of partner's suit. This raise does not show any specific number of points: support for partner can be based on distribution as much as high cards.

These are typical responses of 1 NT to an opening One Spade:

1. ♠ Q 7 4 ♥ J 6 3 ♦ K 9 5 2 ♣ 10 7 6

Just 6 points and about a minimum.

2. ♠ 10 5 ♥ A 8 4 ♦ Q 7 4 2 ♣ K 8 5 4

9 points, close to a maximum for this limited response.

3. ♠ J 4 ♥ K 10 7 5 2 ♦ Q 8 4 ♣ J 5 2

You have a five-card suit and One Heart would be the response to One Diamond or One Club. As we shall see in a moment, a response at the range of Two has to be stronger, so to One Spade respond 1 NT.

The first requirement for a raise of partner's suit is adequate trump support. For a single raise, four small cards or Q x x or sometimes J x x is sufficient. The hand should also contain a short suit elsewhere, a doubleton, singleton or void. These are typical raises of One Heart to Two Hearts:

1. ♠ 6 ♥ K 10 7 4 ♦ J 7 5 3 2 ♣ 6 4 3

Only 4 points, but good trump support and a singleton.

2. ♠ J 7 4 3 ♥ K J 5 ♦ 8 6 ♣ A 5 3 2

Quite strong for a single raise.

3. ♠ 6 4 2 ♥ K Q 6 3 ♦ K 5 2 ♣ 8 4 3

With 4-3-3-3 distribution 1 NT is usually better, but here the strength in hearts points to a raise.

B. Changes of suit that may be quite weak or quite strong

A response at the level of One in a new suit, such as One Heart over One Club, has a wide range, from about 5 points to 15. As a rule, it is better to show a suit at this level, especially a major suit, than to respond 1 NT. It is also better to mention a useful major than to support a minor.

In the following examples partner has opened One Diamond.

First Moves in Bidding

1. ♠ 6 4 ♥ K 10 9 4 2 ♦ 6 5 3 ♣ Q 7 6

Just enough for a response of One Heart. Had partner opened One Spade the choice would have been between 1 NT and No Bid, with preference for the latter.

2. ♠ Q J 10 8 6 4 ♥ 4 ♦ J 7 4 ♣ 10 5 3

It would not be a mistake to pass but most players, with so good a suit, would respond One Spade.

3. ♠ J 5 ♥ A J 9 4 ♦ K 7 6 ♣ 10 5 4 2

Respond One Heart. This is more constructive than supporting diamonds. A minor suit is seldom raised on three trumps. Even if the opening had been One Club it would have been right to bid the hearts.

Before passing on to stronger hands we will test your responses on hands where you must either pass or make a minimum bid.

QUIZ No. 25

Partner has opened One Heart and the next player passes. What do you respond on the following hands?

(101) ♠ Q 8 7 2 ♥ K J 4 ♦ 9 7 4 2 ♣ 10 4

(102) ♠ J 4 ♥ 10 8 3 2 ♦ Q 8 6 4 3 ♣ A 4

(103) ♠ Q 7 4 ♥ 10 6 ♦ K 7 5 ♣ J 8 7 4 2

(104) ♠ J 8 7 5 4 2 ♥ 8 ♦ Q 7 3 2 ♣ J 4

ANSWERS TO QUIZ No. 25

(101) Two Hearts, rather than 1 NT or One Spade on so poor a suit.

(102) Two Hearts, quite a strong raise.

(103) 1 NT. As we shall see in a moment, the hand does not qualify for a response of Two Clubs.

(104) No Bid. You may not like partner's One Heart, but if you bid One Spade you may end up in serious trouble.

QUIZ No. 26

Partner has opened One Club and the next player passes. What do you respond on the following hands?

Opening Suit Bids of One and Responses

(105) ♠ Q 10 8 4   ♥ J 4   ♦ Q 8 5 3   ♣ 10 7 6

(106) ♠ 2   ♥ 10 8 6 4 3   ♦ Q 5 4   ♣ Q J 4 3

(107) ♠ K J 4   ♥ A 9 6   ♦ Q 7 4 2   ♣ 10 9 5

ANSWERS TO QUIZ NO. 26

(105) One Diamond. On moderate hands the general rule is to keep the bidding low.

(106) Two Clubs. Such virtue as this hand possesses lies in the trump support and the singleton spade. If the hand were stronger it would be right to bid One Heart, but here Two Clubs is more prudent.

(107) 1 NT. In response to One Club the limits of 1 NT are slightly higher than in response to any other suit. On a weak hand responder can bid one of the intervening suits. Thus 1 NT is more informative than One Diamond.

We turn now to stronger hands where the response may be at the level of One or Two. Two Diamonds over One Heart, a simple take-out at the level of Two, promises fair values, usually from 9 points upwards.

It is time to mention one of the most important principles in constructive bidding: *a simple change of suit by a player who has not already passed, whether at the level of One or Two, is forcing for one round: the opener will always bid again.*

That is not a rule of the game, of course. It is simply that on balance it pays to have this understanding. Otherwise responder, whenever he had a useful hand, would have to jump the bidding and there would be less room for the exchange of information.

In the following examples partner has opened One Diamond.

1. ♠ K 10 6 4 2   ♥ A K 8 5 3   ♦ 4   ♣ J 2

Respond One Spade. With two five-card suits it is usual to bid the higher ranking. Responder will have an opportunity to show hearts on the next round.

2. ♠ 7 3 2   ♥ A K J 4   ♦ 6 4   ♣ A K 7 6

Respond One Heart. In terms of points, about a maximum for a One-over-One response.

73

3. ♠ A J 9 6 5   ♥ 4   ♦ K 10 7 6   ♣ A 4 2

Respond One Spade. You can show the strong support in diamonds on a later round.

4. ♠ 6 5   ♥ K 8 4   ♦ 3 2   ♣ A J 10 9 7 3

Respond Two Clubs. You have a minimum in high cards for a response at the level of Two, but the suit is strong.

5. ♠ A J 3   ♥ 8 7 4   ♦ Q 5 2   ♣ K J 4 2

Respond Two Clubs, although the suit may seem weak for a response at this level. But partner will bid again, remember; you will have a chance to find a better contract.

C. Encouraging bids, just short of game

A change of suit, as we have just seen, can be either weak or strong. There are two responses that are always quite strong but are nevertheless limited. These are 2 NT and a double raise such as One Heart—Three Hearts.

2 NT is a frequent and effective response on balanced hands containing about 11 to 13 points. In each of the following examples partner has opened One Diamond.

1. ♠ Q 10 6 3   ♥ A J 4   ♦ 6 4   ♣ K Q 6 3

2. ♠ K 5   ♥ A Q 3   ♦ Q 10 7 6   ♣ 10 8 6 3

3. ♠ K Q 4   ♥ K 9   ♦ J 10 4   ♣ K 8 6 4 2

4. ♠ A Q 3   ♥ K 10 6   ♦ J 4 2   ♣ K 5 4 3

There are other possible responses on most of these hands, but since the general strength comes within the 2 NT range, that is the best call.

A double raise of partner's suit, like a single raise, does not show any specific number of points, for distribution is equally important. Approximate requirements are: with four trumps, 9 points and a doubleton or 7 points and a singleton; with three trumps, 9 points and a singleton. In each of the following examples partner has opened One Spade.

1. ♠ J 9 7 4   ♥ 5 3   ♦ A Q 6 3   ♣ K 6 4

You have the values for a raise to Three Spades, and that is a better call than Two Diamonds.

2. ♠ Q 8 6 4 2   ♥ 4   ♦ A 10 6 4 2   ♣ 7 3

Only 6 points, but with five trumps and a singleton a sound raise to Three Spades.

3. ♠ K J 5   ♥ 6 2   ♦ A 8 4 2   ♣ Q 10 6 3

Some players would begin with an approach bid of Two Clubs, but there is nothing wrong with a direct raise to Three Spades.

Double raises in a minor suit are less common because a more constructive bid, such as 2 NT or One of major suit, is usually available. These are two hands on which it would be in order to raise One Diamond to Three Diamonds:

1. ♠ 6   ♥ Q 7 4 3   ♦ A J 10 4   ♣ Q 9 7 2

2. ♠ Q 7 6   ♥ —   ♦ J 8 6 4 3   ♣ K 10 7 4 3

D. Strong bids, forcing at least to game

First, there are the direct game calls—3 NT or a raise of the suit to game level. A response of 3 NT shows a balanced hand of about 14 to 16 points. Partner has opened One Heart and you hold:

1. ♠ K Q 4   ♥ J 7 6   ♦ A Q 9 3   ♣ K 10 4

This 4-3-3-3 distribution is well suited to the response of 3 NT.

2. ♠ K 7 4 2   ♥ Q 5 4   ♦ A 8   ♣ A Q 8 6

Now you have three cards in partner's suit and a doubleton. The hand might develop in a number of ways, and a response of Two Clubs should be preferred to 3 NT.

A raise to game in partner's suit shows at least four trumps and slightly better values than were required for the raise to Three. You would raise One Heart to Four Hearts on hands of this kind:

1. ♠ Q 3   ♥ A Q 8 4   ♦ J 10 7 5 3 2   ♣ 4

2. ♠ K 7 4   ♥ K 10 9 4   ♦ A 8   ♣ Q 6 3 2

3. ♠ 5   ♥ Q 10 8 6 4 2   ♦ 5   ♣ K 8 6 4 3

First Moves in Bidding

A raise to Four or Five of a minor shows always a strong distributional hand. Thus, on hand 1 above, you might raise One Diamond to Five Diamonds.

Finally, we come to very strong hands on which game at least is certain. These are expressed by a jump in a new suit, such as Two Hearts over One Club, or Three Diamonds over One Spade. These responses are unconditionally forcing until game is reached.

Most 16-point hands are worth a forcing response, and when there is exceptional strength in the way of a solid suit or support for partner the force can be made on 12 or 13 points. In the following examples partner has opened One Heart.

1. ♠ A Q J 4 ♥ K 7 6 ♦ A 9 5 2 ♣ J 10

A sound, but not far from minimum, force of Two Spades.

2. ♠ A Q J 10 6 4 ♥ K 6 4 ♦ A 10 6 ♣ 3

Worth a force because of the strong suit.

3. ♠ A Q 7 ♥ 4 ♦ K Q J 6 ♣ Q J 4 3 2

This is a hand on which you will certainly reach game eventually but it does not possess the quality of a force. Moreover, you may need bidding space in which to find the best contract. Respond simply Two Clubs, which as you know is forcing for the present.

4. ♠ A 7 ♥ K Q 8 5 ♦ K 8 7 ♣ A 9 5 3

With 16 points made up of top cards, excellent trump support, and a doubleton, you are too strong for a simple raise to Four Hearts. Rather than leap to Five or Six Hearts you force with Three Clubs and show the heart support on the next round.

Quiz No. 27

Partner has opened One Diamond and the next player passes. What do you respond on the following hands?

(108) ♠ A Q 8 4 ♥ Q 7 6 ♦ 4 ♣ K 10 9 6 2

(109) ♠ K J 10 ♥ K 7 ♦ K 10 7 6 4 ♣ A J 9

(110) ♠ A J 7 2 ♥ K Q 10 5 ♦ 8 ♣ A K 10 7

(111) ♠ K Q J 9 7 6 4 ♥ 5 2 ♦ Q 3 ♣ 6 4

ANSWERS TO QUIZ NO. 27

(108) Two Clubs, bidding the longer suit first.

(109) 3 NT. With a guard in every suit, this is the best tactical bid.

(110) Two Spades, the higher-ranking suit.

(111) Three Spades. This is a type of response that has not so far been described. With a long suit and little in the way of high cards you jump to a high level, mainly to make it difficult for the opponents to bid. Note that Three Spades has an entirely different meaning from Two Spades.

QUIZ NO. 28

Partner has opened One Spade and the next player passes. What do you respond on the following hands?

(112) ♠ A 10 5 3 ♥ K 9 7 4 2 ♦ 3 ♣ K 6 4

(113) ♠ 4 ♥ A J 6 4 ♦ Q 8 5 2 ♣ A 10 7 3

(114) ♠ K J 10 4 ♥ 5 ♦ A Q 9 4 3 ♣ K J 5

(115) ♠ K 7 4 ♥ Q J 8 ♦ J 10 8 5 ♣ A 9 4

ANSWERS TO QUIZ NO. 28

(112) Four Spades, holding 10 points, good trump support and a singleton.

(113) Two Clubs, not 2 NT with a singleton of partner's suit. When responding at the level of Two on four-card suits it is generally better to bid a low-ranking suit, giving partner more room to describe his hand.

(114) Three Diamonds. As you can see by comparing with example (112), you are too strong for a raise to Four Spades.

(115) 2 NT, a better description of your hand than Three Spades.

When there has been an Intervening Call

When there has been an overcall by a defender you will sometimes be prevented from making your natural response. With a moderate hand you may have to pass for the present.

The bidding goes:

South	West	North	East
1 ♦	1 ♠	?	

North holds:

1. ♠ 5 4   ♥ K 10 7 6 3   ♦ 6 4 2   ♣ K 7 3

North would have responded One Heart had there been no intervention. As it would not be sound to call Two Hearts he must pass.

2. ♠ 10 7 4   ♥ Q J 4   ♦ J 7 5   ♣ K 8 4 2

North would have bid 1 NT if West had passed. That is ruled out now both because he is minimum and because he has no guard in spades. He should pass. If he were to bid after the intervention it would be called a 'free' bid.

3. ♠ K J 10 6 5   ♥ K 5 4   ♦ 3   ♣ Q 7 3 2

With such good defence against One Spade North should double, indicating that he sees the chance of obtaining a penalty. The fact that he is short in his partner's suit is a recommendation for the double.

Responding after an Original Pass

When the responder has previously passed and is therefore known to be limited in strength, simple changes of suit are no longer forcing. Thus the bidding goes:

South	West	North	East
No	No	1 ♥	No
2 ♣			

If North has a minimum opening he can pass the response of Two Clubs. The effect of that is that a responder who has passed should avoid tentative and exploratory bids when he has something more definite to proclaim. After North has opened One Heart third in hand, South holds:

1. ♠ 6 5 4   ♥ K 10 4   ♦ K 9 6 4 2   ♣ A 3

Although the trumps are weak for a double raise, it is better to jump to Three Hearts than to respond Two Diamonds.

2. ♠ A J 8   ♥ 6 4   ♦ K 9 6 4   ♣ A 10 8 5

Now prefer 2 NT to an exploratory Two Clubs; but do not fall into the common error of overbidding with 3 NT 'because I had passed, partner'. The fact that a player has passed originally does not make his hand any stronger.

Forcing after a pass

A jump in a new suit is forcing as always, but the strength in high cards is limited by the original pass. The force will generally be based on good support for partner's suit. You hold

♠ A 10 8 6 3   ♥ 5 2   ♦ A Q 6 4   ♣ 7 3

Having passed, respond Two Spades to partner's opening of One Diamond, but only One Spade over One Heart or One Club.

9

The Second Round

The second call made by the opener is known as the 'rebid'. The rebid depends, naturally, on the response, so the best way to tackle this subject is to consider how opener should rebid in face of the various responses described in the last chapter. We examine these rebids in the following order:

1. When partner has responded 1 NT.
2. When partner has responded 2 NT.
3. When partner has given a single raise.
4. When partner has given a double raise.
5. When partner has made a One-over-One response.
6. When partner has made a Two-over-One response.
7. When partner has made a forcing response.

1. The Rebid over a Response of 1 NT

Rebids over a no-trump response are usually straightforward because partner has given a fairly close picture of his hand—6 to 9 points, no useful suit that could be bid at the level of One, and no special support for the suit opened.

To have a prospect of game in no-trumps, you will remember from Chapter 6, you want about 24 to 25 points. On balanced hands therefore, taking partner's average to be 7 or 8, you require about 17 to raise to 2 NT. With 19 you can raise to Three.

With an unbalanced hand containing no second suit you rebid your suit at a minimum level when you have only a fair to moderate hand. When you have a strong hand, jump to Three in your suit. As a rough test, if you can take a King away and still have a sound opening you are probably worth a jump rebid. Thus, you have opened One Heart, partner has responded 1 NT, and you hold:

♠ 5   ♥ A Q 10 7 5 2   ♦ K 7 4   ♣ A J 5

You would have a sound opening without the King of diamonds, so you can suggest game with a jump to Three Hearts.

When you have a fair two-suited hand you show your second suit at a minimum level. A jump in a new suit is forcing, and for this you will need to be at least an Ace better than an opening bid.

QUIZ No. 29

You have opened One Spade and partner has responded 1 NT. What is your rebid on the following hands?

(116) ♠ A Q 8 5 3   ♥ K J 4   ♦ 6 2   ♣ K Q 10

(117) ♠ A J 10 8 4   ♥ 6   ♦ K Q J 7 4   ♣ K 5

(118) ♠ K Q J 8 4 2   ♥ 5   ♦ K J 4 3   ♣ A 6

(119) ♠ K Q J 4   ♥ A Q 6   ♦ Q 8   ♣ A 9 4 2

ANSWERS TO QUIZ No. 29

(116) No Bid. With 15 points you have not enough for 2 NT. Your distribution is well suited to no-trumps, so there is no point in bidding Two Spades, which increases the level of the contract and may not suit partner.

(117) Two Diamonds. The distribution is strong, but you need some encouragement from partner before you can try for game.

(118) Three Spades. There is no point in mentioning the diamonds, for certainly you don't want to be left in Two Diamonds.

(119) 2 NT. The right bid on a balanced 18.

2. The Rebid after a Response of 2 NT

The response of 2 NT, showing 11 to 13 points and a balanced hand, puts the partnership very close to game even when the opening is a minimum. With a balanced hand the opener should pass only when his hand is markedly lacking in playing strength—that is, intermediate cards and long suits.

A rebid in the opener's suit, One Heart—2 NT—Three Hearts, is comparatively discouraging. It says to partner: 'I have opened on a minimum hand with long hearts and unbalanced distribution; maybe this is as high as we should go.' It follows that when the opener expects to make game in his suit he must jump to Four.

Any change of suit is forcing; the 2 NT responder will either support the second suit, bid 3 NT, or show preference for the first suit.

Quiz No. 30

You have opened One Heart and partner has responded 2 NT. What is your rebid on the following hands?

(120) ♠ J 4   ♥ K Q 9 7 6   ♦ A Q 5   ♣ J 4 2

(121) ♠ A 8 7   ♥ A K J 4   ♦ 9 7 5 2   ♣ 6 3

(122) ♠ K 4   ♥ Q J 9 7 5 3   ♦ A K 7   ♣ 6 3

(123) ♠ A 8   ♥ A K 7 4 2   ♦ 5   ♣ K Q 10 7 6

Answers to Quiz No. 30

(120) 3 NT. With 13 points and a five-card suit you have little more than a minimum opening, but with a 12-point hand opposite there should be fair play for game.

(121) No Bid. You have opened this hand because it has top tricks and fair strength in the majors, but you will need a lot from partner to make 3 NT.

(122) Four Hearts. Remember that Three Hearts would be a 'sign-off', as it is called. With your six-card suit you should be able to make game in hearts.

(123) Three Clubs. There may well be a slam, but the change of suit is forcing and there is no need to jump. You can judge your next action according to partner's response.

3. The Rebid after a Single Raise

The single raise, like 1 NT, is a limited response and to try for game you need to be at least a King better than minimum. Thus, with a balanced hand, you need about 17 to suggest game in no-trumps.

Any change of suit is forcing for one round, and a common device is to bid a second suit, not with any intention of playing in that suit, but to see if partner can jump to game, as he should if his original raise was better than minimum.

QUIZ No. 31

You have opened One Diamond and partner has raised to Two Diamonds. What is your rebid on the following hands?

(124) ♠ K Q 7 4 ♥ J 5 ♦ A Q 9 6 3 ♣ Q 2

(125) ♠ 6 3 ♥ A K 4 ♦ A Q 8 6 5 2 ♣ K J

(126) ♠ Q 7 4 ♥ A 3 ♦ A K 10 7 4 2 ♣ K 5

ANSWERS TO QUIZ No. 31

(124) No Bid. There is no prospect of game, for if partner had had a fair hand he would have made a more constructive response than Two Diamonds.

(125) Two Hearts. Hoping to find your way to 3 NT. If partner raises the hearts you can return to diamonds.

(126) 2 NT. Only 16 points, but the diamonds should be solid after the raise. If partner is especially unsuited to game in no-trumps he will sign off in Three Diamonds and then you can pass.

QUIZ No. 32

You have opened One Spade and partner has raised to Two Spades. What is your rebid on the following hands?

(127) ♠ K Q 10 7 6 4 ♥ 5 3 ♦ K Q 4 ♣ A 5

(128) ♠ A Q 6 4 2 ♥ K 7 6 ♦ 5 ♣ A Q 3 2

(129) ♠ K Q J 6 ♥ A 8 5 ♦ A J 4 2 ♣ A 7

ANSWERS TO QUIZ No. 32

(127) Three Spades. Applying the test we mentioned above,

you have a King more than a minimum opening, for if you took the King of diamonds away you would still open One Spade.

(128) Three Clubs. Whether this hand will produce game may depend on the fit—that is to say, on whether partner has his cards in the right place. You do not propose to play in clubs, but you ask partner to give you Four Spades if he has a fair raise and a fit in clubs such as the King. A singleton with good trumps would also be a suitable holding.

(129) Four Spades. You have game values and it is unlikely that you will find a better contract.

4. The Rebid after a Double Raise

When partner raises your major suit from One to Three you will decline the invitation to game only with a minimum opening. Any bid of a new suit at this level is a slam suggestion.

Over Three of a minor you should try for 3 NT on a balanced hand that is a little better than minimum.

5. The Rebid after a One-over-One Response

Partner's response at the level of One (when he has not passed originally) has a wide range, as we noted in the last chapter, from about 5 to 15 points. The opener must never pass because partner may be strong and intending to go to game on the next round. Like responses, rebids can be classified according to general strength.

(a) Minimum rebids that limit the hand

In their different ways the following rebids all suggest an opening bid that is not more than a Queen or so better than minimum:

A rebid of 1 NT, generally 13 to 15 points.

A single raise of partner's suit.

A simple rebid of the opener's suit.

(b) Simple changes of suit that can be quite weak or quite strong

A sequence such as One Club—One Heart—One Spade can vary from a minimum opening to about 18 points.

The Second Round

A sequence such as One Heart—One Spade—Two Clubs has a similar range.

Quiz No. 33

The bidding has gone:

South	West	North	East
1 ♦	No	1 ♥	No
?			

As South, what is your rebid on the following hands?

(130) ♠ J 4 2 ♥ K 7 ♦ A Q 10 7 3 2 ♣ Q 4

(131) ♠ K 7 3 ♥ 10 6 ♦ A K 9 6 2 ♣ A 10 4

(132) ♠ K 4 2 ♥ A 7 6 ♦ K Q 10 7 3 ♣ Q 8

(133) ♠ A J 9 4 ♥ Q 7 2 ♦ A K 6 4 2 ♣ 5

Answers to Quiz No. 33

(130) Two Diamonds.

(131) 1 NT. The diamonds are rebiddable, but 1 NT gives a better picture of the balanced strength.

(132) Two Hearts. Both 1 NT and Two Diamonds are possible calls on the values held, but a sound principle is to give preference to the raise of partner's major suit.

(133) One Spade. Here you are rather strong for a simple raise to Two Hearts. You bid the spades now and show the heart support on the next round.

(c) Encouraging rebids that show better than a minimum opening

In this category are the following:

A rebid of 2 NT, suggesting a balanced hand of 16 to 18 points.

A jump rebid, such as One Diamond—One Spade—Three Diamonds. The main feature of the hand will be long diamonds and the general strength not less than a King better than minimum.

A double raise of partner's suit, One Diamond—One Heart—Three Hearts. The extra strength can lie in either high cards or distribution.

First Moves in Bidding

A bid at the range of Two in a suit of higher rank than the first suit, such as: One Diamond—One Spade—Two Hearts. This type of sequence, known as a 'reverse', has to be stronger because if partner wishes to give preference to the first suit, diamonds, he must go to the level of Three. A reverse suggests upwards of 15 points.

Quiz No. 34

The bidding has gone:

South	West	North	East
1 ♣	No	1 ♠	No
?			

As South, what is your rebid on the following hands?

(134) ♠ Q 4 ♥ A 10 6 ♦ K J 7 ♣ A K 9 6 4

(135) ♠ A 10 8 4 ♥ 6 ♦ A 7 3 ♣ K Q 8 5 2

(136) ♠ 7 3 ♥ A J 4 2 ♦ Q 5 ♣ K Q J 9 3

(137) ♠ K 6 ♥ 4 ♦ A 9 6 2 ♣ A K J 10 5 2

Answers to Quiz No. 34

(134) 2 NT.

(135) Three Spades. Only 13 points in high cards but clearly a useful hand when partner bids spades.

(136) Two Clubs. Two Hearts, a reverse, would be in order if you had the King of hearts instead of the Jack.

(137) Three Clubs.

(d) Rebids that go to game or are forcing to game

A rebid of 3 NT suggests 19 points or more. A raise to game in partner's suit is a natural call, stronger than a jump raise, and in the same way a jump to game in the opener's own suit is stronger than a jump rebid.

A jump bid in a new suit is unconditionally forcing to game. On hands that do not possess exceptional distribution the strength is likely to be 19 points or more.

QUIZ No. 35

The bidding has gone:

South	West	North	East
1 ♥	No	1 ♠	No
?			

As South, what is your rebid on the following hands:

(138) ♠ Q 7   ♥ A K J 4 2   ♦ A Q 5   ♣ K 10 9

(139) ♠ K Q 8 4   ♥ A J 10 5 3   ♦ K Q 4   ♣ 3

(140) ♠ Q J 7 4   ♥ A K 8 6 4 2   ♦ A Q 4   ♣ —

ANSWERS TO QUIZ No. 35

(138) 3 NT.

(139) Four Spades.

(140) Three Diamonds, forcing to game. When you support spades on the next round partner will know that you are short in clubs and will not be worried by losers in that suit.

6. The Rebid after a Two-over-One Response

When partner has responded at the level of Two, the opener's rebids follow much the same pattern as over a response of One, except that a rebid of 2 NT shows better than a minimum hand— about 15 to 17 points.

QUIZ No. 36

The bidding has gone:

South	West	North	East
1 ♥	No	2 ♣	No
?			

As South, what is your rebid on the following hands:

(141) ♠ A 4   ♥ A Q 7 5 3   ♦ J 2   ♣ K Q 6 3

(142) ♠ K 7 4   ♥ A Q 10 6   ♦ K 9 4 3   ♣ J 4

(143) ♠ A J 10   ♥ A K Q 6 3   ♦ K J 8   ♣ 7 3

(144) ♠ Q 4   ♥ A J 10 8 6 3   ♦ K 5   ♣ A 8 4

(141) Four Clubs.

(142) Two Diamonds. A poor suit, but you are under strength for 2 NT and you have to bid something.

(143) 3 NT with all suits well held.

(144) Three Hearts. When partner has bid at the level of Two he shows fair strength and the jump rebid can be made more freely than over a response at the range of One.

7. The Rebid after a Forcing Response

When partner has made a forcing response—a jump in a new suit—the general rule for the opener is to rebid in the same denomination as though partner had made a simple response. If after One Diamond—One Heart he would have bid Two Diamonds, then after One Diamond—Two Hearts he bids Three Diamonds, and so forth. When better than minimum the opener has no need to jump, for once there has been a force both partners are pledged to keep the bidding open to game at least.

The Second Bid by Responder

When the opener makes his rebid he defines his hand within reasonably close limits, and responder should usually be able to judge whether game is unlikely, worth exploring, or surely worth bidding.

The important figure to bear in mind at this stage is that unless tricks can be made from long suits about 25 points are required for game in no-trumps. Therefore, when responder can judge that the combined hands fall short of this figure and that there is no special fit, he must pass or make a minimum bid.

Let us say, first, that opener has made a strictly limited rebid such as 1 NT, a minimum repeat of his suit, or a single raise of responder's suit. The upper limit for all these calls is about 15. With no better than a balanced 9 responder must not try for game and should pass if the present contract suits him reasonably well.

The Second Round

With 10 or 11 he should make some forward-going bid such as 2 NT or a change of suit or a raise of partner's suit. With 12 or more points opposite an opening bid responder should look for game, bidding 3 NT or making a jump of some kind.

Responder's action is not quite so clear when the opener changes the suit, for then the opener's strength can range from 13 to 18 or so. Responder should pass only with a minimum 6 or 7 points and a better fit for partner's second suit than for his first. With 8 or 9 he will usually make a bid at a low level, with 10 or 11 a more constructive bid such as 2 NT, and with 12 or more he will look for game.

PART FOUR

Some Stratagems in Play

10

The Use of Trumps

You will have noted in the last two chapters that much emphasis was laid on the possession of singletons and doubletons in conjunction with trump support. For example, partner having called spades,

♠ K 10 5 4   ♥ 3   ♦ J 7 5 4 2   ♣ A 5 3

represents better support than

♠ K 10 5 4   ♥ K 7 5   ♦ J 4 3   ♣ A 5 3

This chapter shows how declarer makes use of these 'ruffing values', as they are called.

Ruffing in Dummy

When the dummy contains a short suit as well as good trump support, declarer can generally arrive at extra tricks in the trump suit itself. In the following diagram the first of the two hands above is held by North:

Some Stratagems in Play

Dealer, South   Love all

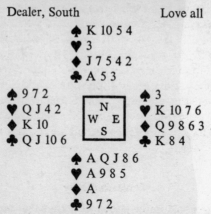

♠ K 10 5 4
♥ 3
♦ J 7 5 4 2
♣ A 5 3

♠ 9 7 2   ♠ 3
♥ Q J 4 2   ♥ K 10 7 6
♦ K 10   ♦ Q 9 8 6 3
♣ Q J 10 6   ♣ K 8 4

♠ A Q J 8 6
♥ A 9 8 5
♦ A
♣ 9 7 2

South opens One Spade, North has a clear raise to Three Spades, and South bids Four.

If he could see all the hands West might lead a trump, but his natural choice is the Queen of Clubs. This lead is both safe and constructive. According to convention, he leads the top card of the sequence, Q J 10.

After the lead of ♣ Q the dummy is displayed and South notes that in top tricks he has five spades in his own hand, together with three Aces. The extra tricks will come easily enough from ruffing hearts with dummy's trumps.

There is no point in holding up the Ace of clubs: that would give the opponents a chance to play trumps, which would not altogether suit the declarer. So the Ace of clubs is played from the table (dummy is often referred to as 'table').

East, on this trick, should drop the 8 of clubs rather than the 4. Any card higher than the 6 will be construed by the other defender as an encouraging signal, asking partner to play the suit when next in the lead.

Having won the first trick with ♣ A, South begins at once to ruff hearts. He leads ♥ 3 to the Ace and returns ♥ 5, ruffing with dummy's ♠ 4. (There is no need to ruff with a high trump, for it is extremely unlikely that East will be out of hearts and able to over-ruff.)

The Use of Trumps

The 4 of spades is returned to the Ace and another heart is ruffed with ♠ 10. Then comes a diamond to the Ace, and the last heart is ruffed with dummy's last trump, the King. South returns to hand by ruffing a diamond with ♠ 8. His remaining trumps are masters and at the finish he concedes two clubs to the opponents. He makes eleven tricks in all—Four Spades with an overtrick.

You will note that the result would be quite different if declarer were to draw three rounds of trumps. Then only one trump would be left in dummy for ruffing hearts, and the contract would in fact be one down.

Cross-Ruff Play

On some hands declarer makes no attempt to draw trumps at all, setting out from the first to make the trumps separately. He is then said to play the hand on a 'cross-ruff'.

Dealer, South   Game all

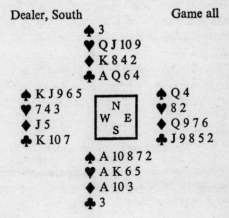

The bidding goes as follows:

South	West	North	East
1 ♠	No	2 ♣	No
2 ♥	No	4 ♥	No
5 ♦	No	6 ♥	No
No	No		

Some Stratagems in Play

After the jump raise in hearts the message of South's Five Diamonds is: 'It looks to me as though we may be able to make a slam in hearts. I control the first round of diamonds. If that is the suit you were worried about, perhaps you can give me Six Hearts?'

From the way that the bidding has gone, and from his own length in spades, the first suit bid by declarer, West judges that declarer will need some ruffs to make the slam in hearts. Accordingly he opens the 3 of hearts, hoping that the defence will come in to lead a second round of trumps later.

Declarer wins the first trick in dummy and sees that the trump opening was indeed a shrewd stroke by the defence. Barring this lead, he would make twelve tricks via four top winners in the side suits, four hearts in dummy, and four in his own hand.

After the trump lead he cannot ruff four spades in dummy. To make the extra trick he must risk the club finesse. The play begins as follows:

Trick 1: 9 of hearts wins in dummy.
Trick 2: spade to Ace.
Trick 3: finesse of ♣ Q wins.

Now South can see daylight. He discards a diamond on ♣ A, cashes two top diamonds, and ruffs a club with ♥ 6. By now he has made seven tricks and has five master trumps left, which he cannot be prevented from making separately.

Establishing a Suit by Ruffing

Another very important function of the trump suit is to enable declarer to establish a side suit by ruffing out the enemy winners. This is a common type of hand:

The Use of Trumps

Dealer, South   N-S vulnerable

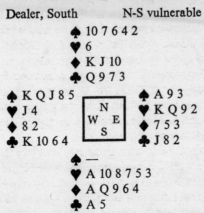

                ♠ 10 7 6 4 2
                ♥ 6
                ♦ K J 10
                ♣ Q 9 7 3

♠ K Q J 8 5   ♠ A 9 3
♥ J 4   ♥ K Q 9 2
♦ 8 2   ♦ 7 5 3
♣ K 10 6 4   ♣ J 8 2

                ♠ —
                ♥ A 10 8 7 5 3
                ♦ A Q 9 6 4
                ♣ A 5

The bidding goes:

South	West	North	East
1 ♥	1 ♠	No	2 ♠
3 ♦	No	4 ♦	No
5 ♦	No	No	No

When South bids up to the level of Three on his own, vulnerable,
North must give him a chance to reach game.

West leads the King of spades (top of a sequence, remember?)
and South ruffs with ♦ 4. It is clear that if he draws trumps he
will not be able to establish the hearts. The first step is ♥ A and
a heart ruff. Now it may seem that declarer can continue with a
cross-ruff, but if you count the tricks you will see that at best he
will make eight tricks in trumps and two Aces. Instead, he must
hope to draw trumps and establish winners in hearts.

A club is led to the Ace and another heart is ruffed. On this
trick West discards a club. South knows—and he shouldn't need
to count—that there is still a master heart against him. In fact the
position is:

Some Stratagems in Play

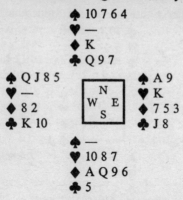

♠ 10 7 6 4
♥ —
♦ K
♣ Q 9 7

♠ Q J 8 5
♥ —
♦ 8 2
♣ K 10

N
W E
S

♠ A 9
♥ K
♦ 7 5 3
♣ J 8

♠ —
♥ 10 8 7
♦ A Q 9 6
♣ 5

The lead is in dummy and South could make a bad mistake now by coming to hand with a spade ruff and trumping the last heart. The hearts would be good then but South would not be able to draw trumps. He would have lost control, in the technical phrase. Instead, he should overtake ♦ K with the Ace, draw the trumps and concede a heart. He still has a trump left and all he loses is one heart and one club.

Equally common is the establishment by ruffing of a suit in dummy. In this example South has to be careful about the entries:

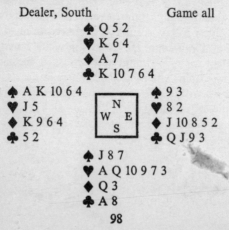

Dealer, South   Game all

♠ Q 5 2
♥ K 6 4
♦ A 7
♣ K 10 7 6 4

♠ A K 10 6 4
♥ J 5
♦ K 9 6 4
♣ 5 2

N
W E
S

♠ 9 3
♥ 8 2
♦ J 10 8 5 2
♣ Q J 9 3

♠ J 8 7
♥ A Q 10 9 7 3
♦ Q 3
♣ A 8

The Use of Trumps

The bidding goes:

South	West	North	East
1 ♥	1 ♠	2 ♣	No
2 ♥	No	3 ♥	No
4 ♥	No	No	No

The traditional lead from a suit headed by the Ace-King is the King. That is an exception to the general practice of leading the top card of a sequence.

West leads the King of spades, therefore, and on this trick East plays the 9. That is an encouraging card, known as a 'peter'; East places his partner with ♠ A K and plans to ruff dummy's Queen on the third round.

When he sees the 9 of spades West follows with the Ace. East completes his peter and West plays a third spade, which East ruffs. East now switches to the Jack of diamonds. Not very hopefully South puts in the Queen, and this is headed by the King and Ace.

South has lost three tricks and his problem now is to dispose of the loser in diamonds. That can be done only if he can develop a trick in clubs. After one round of trumps the following cards are left:

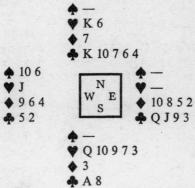

It would be a mistake to lead another trump at this point because the two entries to dummy may be needed later. The play continues:

99

Some Stratagems in Play

Trick 6: Ace of clubs.

Trick 7: low club to the King.

Trick 8: club from dummy, ruffed by the Queen. There is only one trump outstanding, so declarer must not risk being over-ruffed.

Trick 9: 9 of hearts to dummy's King. Note that South is retaining the 3 of hearts, for later he will want to cross to dummy's 6.

Trick 10: fourth round of clubs ruffed by ♥ 10. This extracts the last club from East.

Trick 11: 3 of hearts to dummy's 6.

Trick 12: 10 of clubs from dummy, South discarding ♦ 3.

Trick 13: won by South's last heart.

Tricks at the Right Time

The art of play consists not merely of winning tricks but of winning them at the right moment. At no-trumps especially a controlling card may be held up for two or three rounds.

Hold-Up Play

The play at no-trumps often develops into a struggle between the two sides to establish and run their respective long suits. Observe how on the following hand declarer succeeds by holding up his winning card in the enemy suit.

Dealer, North   Love all

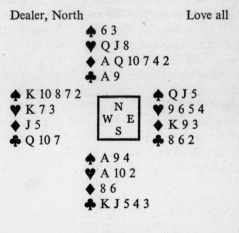

```
                    ♠ 6 3
                    ♥ Q J 8
                    ♦ A Q 10 7 4 2
                    ♣ A 9
    ♠ K 10 8 7 2           ♠ Q J 5
    ♥ K 7 3          N     ♥ 9 6 5 4
    ♦ J 5         W   E    ♦ K 9 3
    ♣ Q 10 7         S     ♣ 8 6 2
                    ♠ A 9 4
                    ♥ A 10 2
                    ♦ 8 6
                    ♣ K J 5 4 3
```

Some Stratagems in Play

The bidding goes:

South	West	North	East
—	—	1 ♦	No
2 ♣	No	2 ♦	No
2 NT	No	3 NT	No
No	No		

It is usually sound tactics for the defenders against a no-trump contract to begin with their longest suit. The conventional lead, except when a strong combination of honours is held, is the fourth card from the top. In the present instance, therefore, West leads the 7 of spades. Dummy plays the 3 and East the Jack, for while the top card of a sequence is *led*, the lowest card is *played*.

Since spades are the danger suit, and he does not mind conceding the first two tricks, declarer holds up his Ace on this trick. The importance of that will be seen later.

East continues spades, leading the Queen. Unless there is a good reason to do something different it is generally sound play for the defence to continue the suit originally led. South holds off again and wins the third spade with the Ace. On this trick he has to discard from dummy. The diamonds are valuable, so he lets go a heart.

South has hopes of making five tricks in diamonds: that will be possible if the honours are divided and the suit breaks 3-2. To the fourth trick he leads ♦ 6. West plays low and the 10 is played from dummy—a double finesse.

Since his King is twice guarded East might hold off this trick. That is often good play for the defence as well. On the present occasion, however, to hold off could be a mistake from East's point of view: declarer might be able to run for home. East's natural defence is to take the King of diamonds and lead a heart, hoping that his partner will come in to make two winning spades.

South has no reason to risk the heart finesse, for he sees that provided the diamonds break he will score game by way of five diamonds and four top winners in the other suits. He puts on the Ace of hearts, therefore, and leads another diamond. When both opponents follow, game is assured.

Tricks at the Right Time

It is easy to see that the result would have been quite different had South won the first or second round of spades. Then East would have had a spade to lead to his partner when he came in with ♦ K, and the defence would have made four tricks in spades and one in diamonds.

Ducking Play

Another time when declarer will decline to take a trick is when he wants to maintain communication with the opposite hand. The manœuvre in diamonds on the following hand is known as 'ducking play'.

Dealer, South   Game all

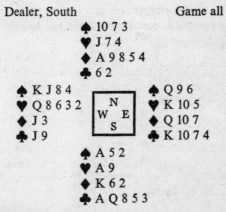

```
              ♠ 10 7 3
              ♥ J 7 4
              ♦ A 9 8 5 4
              ♣ 6 2
♠ K J 8 4                      ♠ Q 9 6
♥ Q 8 6 3 2        N           ♥ K 10 5
♦ J 3          W     E         ♦ Q 10 7
♣ J 9             S            ♣ K 10 7 4
              ♠ A 5 2
              ♥ A 9
              ♦ K 6 2
              ♣ A Q 8 5 3
```

The bidding goes:

South	West	North	East
1 ♣	No	1 ♦	No
2 NT	No	No	No

West leads fourth best of his long suit—the 3 of hearts. Declarer plays low from dummy and East puts in the 10. It is true that by so doing he may, for all he knows, be allowing South to win a trick with the Queen, but in that case South will have the suit guarded in any event. This kind of finesse by the defence against an honour visible on the table is normal play. To put on

103

the King of hearts would clearly be a mistake here, for it would establish dummy's Jack as a second stop.

When the 10 of hearts is played South has to decide whether to take the trick or to hold up the Ace. It would be wrong to hold up on this occasion, for playing in 2 NT declarer can afford to lose four heart tricks and certainly he would not welcome a switch to spades by the defence.

South takes ♥ A, therefore, and plays ♦ K followed by ♦ 6. This is where he makes the critical play. He ducks in dummy, allowing the defenders to win this trick. The opponents may cash their heart winners now, but as soon as they play a spade South goes up with the Ace and uses his last diamond to cross to dummy's Ace and make the good diamonds on the table. South still needs the club finesse for his contract. When that succeeds, he is home with four diamonds, two clubs and two Aces.

Ducking play is equally common in defence. It is worth bearing in mind that the mechanics of the game are just the same whichever side plays the hand.

Dealer, South   Love all

```
                        ♠ Q J 10 8 5
                        ♥ J 7 2
                        ♦ 7 3
                        ♣ A Q 6
        ♠ A 7 3 2                        ♠ 9 6
        ♥ 6 3            N                ♥ A K 8 5 4
        ♦ K 10 6 4    W     E             ♦ J 8
        ♣ J 8 4          S                ♣ 10 7 3 2
                        ♠ K 4
                        ♥ Q 10 9
                        ♦ A Q 9 5 2
                        ♣ K 9 5
```

The bidding goes:

South	West	North	East
1 ♦	No	1 ♠	No
1 NT	No	2 NT	No
3 NT	No	No	No

On this occasion both West's long suits, such as they are, have been bid against him. He might lead a low club, but we will say instead that he chooses a heart, partly because that lead will give nothing away and partly in the hope of finding partner with strong hearts.

While admiring his partner's intuition, East must be careful to duck on this lead, playing an encouraging card, the 8. East can be sure from the bidding that partner's ♥ 6 is 'top of nothing', as it is called. It could not be fourth best, from Q 10 9 6, both because the 10 is the right lead from that holding and because that would leave declarer with just the singleton 3.

South wins the first trick and plays on spades. His only hope is that the hearts will be divided 4-3. But when West comes in with ♠ A he has another heart to lead to his partner and East makes four heart tricks to defeat the contract.

Another time when ducking play is essential in defence is when a suit is distributed in this fashion:

J 4

K 9 7 5 2   A 8 3

Q 10 6

Defending against no-trumps, West leads the 5, East wins with the Ace and returns the 8. Now if he has no side entry West must hold off, leaving his partner with another card to lead. (If East had held four cards, e.g. A 8 6 3, his correct return would have been the fourth best, the 3.)

It is the same when a suit is divided 4-3-3-3, as in this diagram:

10 4 2

Q 9 6 3   K 8 7

A J 5

Here South has a double stop. West leads the 3, dummy plays low and the King is headed by the Ace. When the defenders next have the lead West must hold up his Queen. Declarer wins a second trick in the suit, but East retains the 8 to lead to his partner's Q 9.

12

Defensive Measures

The opening lead presents a problem in two parts: which suit will you lead, and which card of that suit? We have to consider suit and no-trump contracts separately, for quite different considerations arise.

The Lead at No-Trumps

We have already noted that the play at no-trumps often develops into a struggle between the opposing sides to establish their long suits. That is why, for the most part, the defender leads from his longest and strongest suit.

The most attractive lead, if you have the cards for it, is from a four-card or longer suit headed by a strong combination of honours such as K Q J or Q J 10. From holdings of this sort the top card is led. There are several reasons for this, the most important being that you don't want to give declarer the chance to win an easy trick with a lower card. For example, the distribution may be:

6 4 2

K Q J 8   9 5 3

A 10 7

Obviously it would not be clever to lead the 8 and allow declarer to win a trick with the 10.

Another reason for leading a high card from a strong honour combination is so that you retain a low card when your partner has length. For example:

K 4

Q J 9 7   8 6 5 3 2

A 10

106

You see what would happen if you were to lead the 7 instead of the Queen? You would clear the suit in two leads, but you would not be able to put your partner in to make the fifth card. The suit would be 'blocked'.

It will be seen from the table which follows that the general rule is to lead the top of a sequence or the higher of touching honours, an exception being that the King is led from A K.

From a suit headed by:

A K Q	lead	K
A K J	,,	K
A Q J	,,	Q
A J 10	,,	J
K Q J	,,	K
K Q 10	,,	K
Q J 10	,,	Q
Q J 9	,,	Q
J 10 9	,,	J
J 10 8	,,	J
A 10 9	,,	10
K 10 9	,,	10
Q 10 9	,,	10
10 9 8	,,	10

You also lead the 9 from a combination such as 9 8 7 x, or the 8 from 8 7 6 x. For the rest, the standard lead is fourth best—the fourth card from the top. That is especially important from a holding such as A K x x x when you have no side entry, for the distribution may be of this order:

$$J 7 4$$
$$A K 9 5 2 \qquad\qquad 8 3$$
$$Q 10 6$$

By starting with the low card, the 5, you leave your partner with a card to return should he be next in the lead. In effect you are practising the ducking play described in the last chapter.

Choosing from suits of equal length

Very often you will have two suits of equal length, neither of which has been called by the opposition. As between two five-card suits, you will not be far wrong if you open the stronger. As between four-card suits, however, you should generally look for the lead that is less likely to give away a trick. It is not pleasant to lead away from A Q 10 x, almost certainly presenting the declarer with an easy trick: much better to lead a safe 9 from 9 8 7 x.

The lead from a short suit

There are times when the lead from your long suit will seem especially unattractive. An obvious occasion is when the suit has been called by an opponent. Another time is when you have a specially weak hand. For example, opponents bid 1 NT—2 NT— 3 NT, and you have to lead from:

♠ Q 5 4   ♥ 7 3   ♦ 9 7 6 4 2   ♣ J 7 6

Because of your lack of entries and the weakness of the suit, you haven't much chance of beating 3 NT by leading diamonds: better to play for your partner's hand by leading a spade or heart. If you decided on a spade (or club) you would lead the bottom card from three to an honour; if a heart, you would lead the higher card from a doubleton, trusting partner to recognize the 7 as 'top of nothing' rather than fourth best.

The lead when partner has bid

When partner has bid a suit and the opponents have contracted for no-trumps over it, you should generally lead his suit, especially when he has made an overcall rather than an opening bid, and most of all when he has overcalled at the level of Two, suggesting a fairly good suit. Do not argue along the lines: 'They have bid 3 NT over his suit, they must hold it pretty well, I'll lead my own suit instead.' As we shall see in Chapter 14, one of the objects of defensive bidding is to tell partner what to lead against no-trumps, and it is annoying to risk an overcall for that reason and then see partner go off on some goose chase of his own.

When leading partner's suit, the standard plays are as follows:

Defensive Measures

From	8 5	lead	8
,,	8 5 3	,,	8
,,	8 5 3 2	,,	2
,,	Q 5	,,	Q
,,	Q J 7	,,	Q
,,	Q 10 7	,,	7
,,	Q 7 3	,,	3
,,	Q 8 7 4	,,	4

This list is not comprehensive but it shows the general principle —low from four cards or three cards headed by an honour. The object of leading low from three to an honour is to trap a high card held by the declarer. The distribution may be:

5

K 10 2   Q 9 7 6 4 3

A J 8

It is apparent that if West leads the King declarer will have a double stop, but if West leads the 2 then declarer's Jack can be trapped by a lead from East towards the K 10. There are many similar combinations.

The Lead against a Suit Contract

In a suit contract there is not as a rule any special advantage in leading from length. It does not help to establish a suit when declarer has several trumps and can afford to ruff.

The best lead is one that is both safe and constructive. A short and strong sequence such as K Q J or Q J 10 is ideal.

Another good lead is a long suit headed by A K. The King is led, not the fourth best as at no-trumps. Study these two situations:

(i)   (ii)

J 7 4   J 7 4

A K 8 5 2   10 3   A K 8 5   Q 10 3

Q 9 6   9 6 2

West leads the King and on both occasions East peters with the 10 to show that he is ready for the suit to be continued. In example

Some Stratagems in Play

(i) this leads to a ruff on the third round; in example (ii) the defence makes the first three tricks in top cards.

Similarly, from K Q x x x or Q J x x, the top card is led, not the fourth best. From any long suit headed by the Ace it is advisable to lead the Ace as otherwise declarer may make a singleton King (or may win with the King when he has a singleton in the opposite hand). In short, when leading against a suit contract you go for quick tricks rather than slow ones.

The lead from a short suit

A lead from three small cards is less likely to give away a trick than a lead from an honour card and is often preferred for that reason. A lead from a doubleton, still more from a singleton, has the additional advantage that it may lead to a ruff if partner has the Ace or if he can gain the lead before trumps have been drawn.

More hazardous, but sometimes effective, is the lead of the high card from A x, K x, Q x, or J x. This type of lead can cost a trick but it can be highly successful when partner has the cards to fill in.

Trump leads

It is not uncommon to lead a trump for reasons of safety—in preference, that is, to leading from any combination of honours. In addition, the trump lead may prevent declarer from obtaining ruffs in dummy or from developing a cross-ruff. The hand on page 95 was an example.

Playing a Forcing Game

Finally, there is one time when a lead from a long suit is indicated: that is when a defender has long trumps and hopes that if declarer is forced to ruff several times he will run short of trumps. Thus, suppose that the contract is Four Spades and you hold:

♠ Q 6 5 4   ♥ 5 4   ♦ A J 9 5 3   ♣ A 4

If you judge that declarer has five or six trumps and dummy not more than two your best defence will be to lead, not one of your

110

doubletons, but from your long suit in the hope of establishing what is known as a 'force' game. This is the full hand:

Dealer, South   Game all

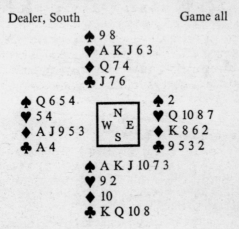

```
                    ♠ 9 8
                    ♥ A K J 6 3
                    ♦ Q 7 4
                    ♣ J 7 6
   ♠ Q 6 5 4                       ♠ 2
   ♥ 5 4            N              ♥ Q 10 8 7
   ♦ A J 9 5 3    W   E            ♦ K 8 6 2
   ♣ A 4            S              ♣ 9 5 3 2
                    ♠ A K J 10 7 3
                    ♥ 9 2
                    ♦ 10
                    ♣ K Q 10 8
```

The bidding goes:

South	West	North	East
1 ♠	No	2 ♥	No
3 ♠	No	4 ♠	No
No	No		

As West, you lead the Ace of diamonds because your general plan is to make the declarer ruff so that your own trumps will take command later on. On the Ace of diamonds your partner plays the 6 as a small encouragement and you see the 10 fall from declarer.

You follow with ♦ J. Declarer plays low from dummy, East plays the 2, completing his encouraging signal, and South ruffs. Declarer's natural continuation is to lay down one top trump, the Ace, and then to cross to dummy's ♥ A to lead another spade.

When East shows void on the second spade, discarding a club, South cannot gain by finessing. He goes up with the King and the position is now:

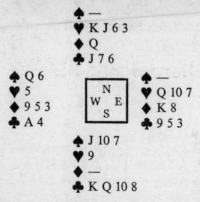

On the surface South has only two losers, but in fact he has lost control of the trump situation. His best play at this point is to force out the Ace of clubs. West wins and forces again in diamonds. South ruffs and continues clubs, allowing West to make his two trump tricks. That is one down, South losing two spades, a diamond and a club.

If you look again at the second diagram you will see that declarer fares even worse if he leads Jack of spades. West wins and plays a diamond, South ruffing. South can draw the last trump now, but when West comes in with ♣ A he will have two more diamonds to make. One can say in general that when a forcing game is practical at all it is the best defence.

PART FIVE

More about Bidding

13

Opening Bids of More than One

Except for a brief look at opening bids of 2 NT and 3 NT, we have so far considered opening bids of One only. The majority of hands, at least four in five, are in fact opened at this level. In general, the lower the bidding starts the more time there is to exchange information and arrive at the best contract.

However, some hands have to be differently treated, either because they are so powerful that one does not want to risk being passed out in a bid of One, or because their virtue is so much concentrated in one suit that it is good tactics to bid high in that suit right away.

We will consider the strong bids first. These are of two kinds—the Strong Two and the conventional Two Clubs.

Two Diamonds, Two Hearts, and Two Spades

These openings are strong but not forcing.* In terms of points (not that points are a reliable method of valuation for this sort of call) you will generally have about 18 to 22, counting as before 2 points for a good six-card suit and 1 for each good five-card suit. These are some examples:

1.   ♠ A Q J 8 6 4   ♥ K 5   ♦ A K J 7 5   ♣ —

Clearly a fine hand, with 18 points in top cards and two good suits. Open Two Spades.

* The reader will appreciate that in matters of this sort there are many different styles of bidding. We describe here a method that is both sound and simple. It is easy to adjust one's bidding to a partner who, for example, plays Two bids as forcing for one round—T.R.

2. ♠ 4 2   ♥ A K J 9 3   ♦ A J 3   ♣ A Q J

Not quite so strong in terms of playing values, but the 20 points, including three Aces, make the hand worth Two Hearts.

3. ♠ A K Q 4   ♥ A Q J 3   ♦ K Q 10 9   ♣ 7

It is rare to open with a Two bid on a four-card suit, but on this hand Two Spades is as good as any of the alternatives.

Two Clubs

Hands that are stronger still are opened with an artificial bid of Two Clubs. That, of course, is a convention, but a very common one which most partners will know.

This bid of Two Clubs is forcing to game with one exception. Partner's first response on a weak hand, as we shall see below, is Two Diamonds. If over Two Diamonds the opener rebids 2 NT, then the partner can pass when extremely weak, holding less than 3 points.

As a rough guide, to qualify for Two Clubs a hand should contain 20 points in high cards plus strong distribution, or a balanced 23 points. But the real test is whether you have practically game in your own hand. These are some examples:

1. ♠ A J 5   ♥ A K Q 7 5 2   ♦ —   ♣ A Q 9 5

Only 20 points in high cards, but clearly you want very little from partner. Open Two Clubs.

2. ♠ 3   ♥ A K J 4   ♦ A K 6   ♣ A Q 10 4 2

Not a sure game hand, but on balance worth Two Clubs since the alternatives, Two Hearts and One Club, are unsatisfactory. Over a response of Two Diamonds you will rebid Two Hearts rather than Three Clubs.

3. ♠ A J 10   ♥ K 10   ♦ A K Q 10 3   ♣ A J 7

Now you open Two Clubs and rebid 2 NT, which partner can pass on a worthless hand,

QUIZ No. 37

What is your opening bid on the following hands?

(145) ♠ K Q J 9 6 4   ♥ Q J 4   ♦ —   ♣ K Q 5 4

(146) ♠ A 8   ♥ Q 6   ♦ A K J 10 7 4   ♣ A K 5

(147) ♠ Q 4   ♥ K 7 6 3 2   ♦ A K Q   ♣ K Q J

(148) ♠ A Q   ♥ K Q 7 4   ♦ A K J 6   ♣ K J 4

ANSWERS TO QUIZ No. 37

(145) One Spade. A powerful hand in its way, but it would be both unsound and unnecessary to open with a Two bid on a hand containing no Ace.

(146) Two Diamonds. Two Clubs would not be a mistake, but by opening Two Diamonds you save a round of bidding as compared with the sequence: Two Clubs (conventional)—Two Diamonds (negative response)—Three Diamonds.

(147) One Heart. An example that shows the hollowness of valuation by point count. You have 20 points but they are not powerfully distributed and you will not make game if partner cannot respond to One Heart.

(148) Two Clubs, and rebid 2 NT.

Responding to Two Bids

When partner has opened with a Two bid the first point to bear in mind is that one reason why he has opened with a bid of Two is that he did not want to risk your passing a bid of One. You should therefore keep the bidding open on less than when responding to a One bid. The weakest response, though it may also be made on a fair hand, is 2 NT.

Partner has opened Two Hearts and you hold:

1. ♠ J 5 2   ♥ 7 3   ♦ Q 7 6 4   ♣ J 8 5 3

Respond 2 NT. If partner rebids Three Hearts you can pass.

2. ♠ J 4   ♥ 7 6 4   ♦ A 8 7   ♣ Q 6 4 3 2

More About Bidding

Of three possible calls, Three Hearts, Three Clubs and 2 NT, the raise to Three Hearts is best. Three small cards represent adequate trump support, though it must be said that some partners demand an honour for an immediate raise.

3. ♠ A 7 4   ♥ Q 8 3   ♦ K 6 4   ♣ Q 7 3 2

This is a strong hand opposite a Two Bid and you will almost surely finish in a slam. To begin with, set the suit with a raise to Three Hearts.

Responding to Two Clubs

The weakness response, as we have already noted, is Two Diamonds. For a positive response you require about 7 points when you can bid a suit at the range of Two, upward of 8 points for 2 NT or a bid at the level of Three.

Partner has opened Two Clubs and you hold:

1. ♠ 10 3   ♥ Q 7 6 5 4 2   ♦ Q 5 2   ♣ J 3

Respond Two Diamonds. You have a good suit but are short of high cards for a positive response.

2. ♠ K Q 10 4 2   ♥ 9 5   ♦ 8 6 4 3   ♣ Q 4

A minimum for a response of Two Spades.

3. ♠ 7 4 2   ♥ Q 10 3   ♦ Q 7 3 2   ♣ K 9 4

With no Ace and only one King the first response should be Two Diamonds rather than 2 NT.

QUIZ No. 38

With West the dealer, how should the bidding go on the following hands?

(149)
	West		East
♠	A Q 10 8 4	♠	J 7 2
♥	3	♥	Q 8 6 4
♦	A K 6 3 2	♦	10 5
♣	A J	♣	Q 7 6 3

(150)	West	East
	♠ A K Q 10 9	♠ 5 2
	♥ 4	♥ 10 7 3
	♦ A K J 4	♦ 8 5
	♣ A Q 3	♣ J 10 7 6 5 2

(151)	West	East
	♠ A K 4	♠ J 8 5 3
	♥ K 4	♥ A Q 8 2
	♦ A K 7 3	♦ 10 5 2
	♣ A Q J 9	♣ 8 3

ANSWERS TO QUIZ No. 38

(149)	West	East
	2 ♠	2 NT[1]
	3 ♦	4 ♠[2]
	No[3]	

[1] East has adequate trump support for a raise but as he has no Ace or King it is advisable to bid 2 NT on the first round.

[2] Now East must 'catch up'. Three Spades would not be forcing and East has enough to play for game.

[3] West knows that his partner is limited, so has no thoughts of slam. Even Four Spades is not a certainty.

(150)	West	East
	2 ♣	2 ♦
	2 ♠	3 ♣[1]
	3 ♦	3 ♠[2]
	4 ♣[3]	5 ♣
	No[4]	

[1] Having made the weakness response of Two Diamonds on the previous round, East can afford now to show a six-card suit.

[2] As he has no guard in hearts and can hardly repeat the clubs, East keeps the bidding alive with a minimum preference for partner's first suit.

[3] West realizes that a heart lead and continuation, reducing him to only four trumps, may be awkward in spades. He therefore gives partner the chance to play in clubs.

[4] It is tempting to bid Six, but West remembers that his partner had made a series of minimum bids and may be very weak. The slam requires rather more than the club finesse, for if the defence begins with two rounds of hearts West's trumps are shortened to A Q alone and he cannot pick up South's ♣ K x x.

(151)   *West*   *East*
          2 ♣   2 ♥
          2 NT[1]   3 NT[2]
          No

[1] West was going to make this bid over a negative Two Diamonds and it is still the best way to express his hand.

[2] East has nothing more to contribute. It is uncommon but, as we see in this example, quite practicable to stay out of a slam after a positive response.

Opening Bids of Three and Four

Opening bids of Three and Four have an entirely different meaning from bids of Two. They are pre-emptive in purpose. That is to say, they are made with the object of buying the contract before the opponents have had a chance to get together.

Suppose that neither side is vulnerable and that as dealer you pick up:

♠ 6 3   ♥ A Q J 10 7 4 2   ♦ 6   ♣ 7 5 3

This would not be a sound opening bid of One, still less of Two, but it is a typical Three bid. If the remaining strength is divided equally round the table you will just about make Three Hearts or perhaps be one down. And suppose you are doubled in Three Hearts and partner does not contribute a single trick? Well, you will be three down doubled, less 100 for honours, losing 400 on balance, but meanwhile you will have saved an adverse game (worth at least 400) and quite possibly a slam (worth nearly 1,000). So you won't have done any damage, and very often your bid will create difficulties for the opposition.

Opening bids of Three are normally made on hands whose high-card strength does not justify a bid of One. Bids of Four, especially in a major suit, can be stronger. In this department of bidding both vulnerability and position at the table, which so far we have been able to ignore, are important considerations. These are some examples:

1. ♠ A K J 9 6 5 4 2   ♥ 2   ♦ Q 7 4   ♣ 3

You can count the spades as worth seven to eight tricks. This is a solid Four Spade opening at any score and in any position at the table.

2. ♠ 7 4   ♥ 5   ♦ J 6 3   ♣ K Q J 9 7 5 3

This is a weak Three bid of a type often made by good players. Some would say that we were wrong to recommend such a gambit to learners, but one might answer that the less experienced the company the greater the value of such defensive calls. That is because it is not at all easy for opponents to arrive at their best contract after an opening at this level. On the present hand, therefore, we recommend an opening Three Clubs not vulnerable in first or third position at the table, but not in second position when one opponent has already passed and partner is more likely to have a good hand; and obviously not in fourth position when you would be happy to throw in.

3. ♠ 4   ♥ A K Q 10 6 4 2   ♦ K J 9   ♣ Q 6

On a stronger hand such as this there is a risk of a different sort in opening with a pre-emptive Four Hearts. The risk is that partner will take you for less and will pass when a slam could be made. For that reason, first or second in hand you should open One Heart. Third or fourth in hand, with a partner who has passed, the chance of missing a slam is much less and you must consider a different aspect: if you open One Heart you give opponents a chance to get together and perhaps arrive at a profitable sacrifice. You should therefore be more inclined to open Four Hearts, especially when vulnerable against not vulnerable.

QUIZ No. 39

As dealer, with neither side vulnerable, what would you call on the following hands?

More About Bidding

(152) ♠ K Q 7 4   ♥ 8   ♦ A Q J 8 6 5 2   ♣ 4

(153) ♠ 7 6   ♥ 4   ♦ J 2   ♣ K Q J 7 6 5 4 3

(154) ♠ K 10 8 6 4 2   ♥ 5   ♦ A 7 6 5 3   ♣ 3

(155) ♠ A J 10 8 7 5 3   ♥ 6   ♦ Q 10 8 5   ♣ 4

ANSWERS TO QUIZ No. 39

(152) One Diamond. There are two reasons why you should not pre-empt in diamonds: one is that you are strong in high cards for Three or Four Diamonds, the other that your hand is well playable in spades should partner have five cards of that suit.

(153) Four Clubs. You can reckon that you have about seven playing tricks. Not vulnerable you are entitled to overbid by three tricks; vulnerable, you would bid only Three Clubs.

(154) No Bid. The spades are too weak and broken for a pre-empt. It is better to await events; you may be able to enter the bidding later on.

(155) Three Spades. You are relatively strong for this call, but the spades are not quite good enough for Four Spades.

Responding to Three Bids

When you are playing with a partner who makes the kind of weak Three bids described in the last section, you need three Aces or about 14 points including two Aces and a King before you can think about disturbing his bid. Aces are especially important because partner will usually have one or more singletons, so that Kings and Queens are often wasted. Vulnerability is again important, but in the opposite way to the opening bid: since partner will be stronger you can raise more freely when vulnerable than when not vulnerable.

QUIZ No. 40

Neither side is vulnerable and the bidding has gone:

South	West	North	East
3 ♥	No	?	

Opening Bids of More than One

What should North bid on the following hands?

(156) ♠ 7 4 2   ♥ 5   ♦ A K 10 7 5 4   ♣ K Q J

(157) ♠ A 9 7 4 2   ♥ 8 3   ♦ A K 7 4   ♣ Q 7

(158) ♠ A J 4 3   ♥ 6 2   ♦ Q 10 7   ♣ A J 5 2

ANSWERS TO QUIZ No. 40

(156) No Bid. You have not enough for Four Hearts and it would be a mistake to 'fight' partner's pre-empt by calling Four Diamonds. Any change of suit would be forcing.

(157) Four Hearts. You have enough in high cards to raise and there is no point in mentioning either of your own suits. If you were to bid Three Spades, for example, that would suggest that you regarded Four Spades as an alternative contract.

(158) No Bid. The odds are against Four Hearts, still more against 3 NT. Had partner been vulnerable you might have raised, expecting Four Hearts to be close.

14

Defensive Overcalls

For overcalling, high cards are not so important as they are for opening bids. Often you are not so much concerned to reach game yourself as to prevent the enemy from reaching game. If you can harass them without risking a big penalty then your overcall is largely justified.

Simple Overcalls

Suppose that the opponent on your right opens One Club and you hold:

♠ K J 10 7 6 4   ♥ 5   ♦ J 9 4 2   ♣ 7 3

Not a great hand in any respect, but an overcall of One Spade is sound tactics. Among the aims that this call may achieve are:

1. It may lead to a profitable sacrifice in Four Spades against an opposing Four Hearts.

2. By calling this suit you may prevent opponents from reaching 3 NT.

3. Suppose that they do reach 3 NT and your partner has the lead, you will have shown him a good line of attack.

4. It is possible that you may arrive at a successful contract in spades.

5. A more subtle point: by intervening with One Spade over One Club you leave opponents with less space in which to develop their auction.

One further consideration is that if you end up in One Spade or Two Spades doubled and lose 300 or so you can be sure that you

Defensive Overcalls

have saved a game. The *wrong* sort of hand on which to make a borderline overcall is one that contains defensive tricks but is not proof against bad distribution. For example, at game all East opens One Spade and as South you hold:

♠ J 10 6 4   ♥ 5   ♦ A Q 4   ♣ K J 8 6 3

This is a most unsuitable hand on which to overcall at the Two level, for these reasons:

    1. Should you be doubled in Two Clubs you could easily go four or five down vulnerable, losing 1,100 or more.

    2. Meanwhile you might not even be saving a game, for you have promising defence against spades and your partner may well hold length in hearts.

As these two examples will have shown, the strength in high cards by no means determines whether one should overcall or not. Simple overcalls at the range of One or Two generally fall within the range of about 5 to 14. As we shall see in the next chapter, there is a separate technique for overcalling on strong hands.

Always you have to consider: does the overcall stand to achieve anything and is it reasonably safe? How those questions are answered is best illustrated by the examples that follow.

Quiz No. 41

    At love all the bidding begins:

South	West	North	East
1 ♦	?		

What should West bid on the following hands?

(159)   ♠ Q 9 7   ♥ K 8 4   ♦ Q J 7 3   ♣ A 10 6

(160)   ♠ A K J 4   ♥ 7 3   ♦ 6 2   ♣ Q 10 7 4 2

(161)   ♠ 4   ♥ A J 8 4   ♦ K 5 2   ♣ K Q J 9 3

Answers to Quiz No. 41

    (159) No Bid. On moderate balanced hands of this sort, especially when tricks are held in the enemy suit, nothing is gained by intervening. If partner can enter the auction then you can jump in No-Trumps.

(160) One Spade. More prudent than overcalling at the level of Two on the weak suit. You would be most uncomfortable if Two Clubs were doubled.

(161) Two Clubs. You are strong enough now to make the natural bid according to the length of the suits, and a further possible advantage of Two Clubs is that you prevent North from responding One Spade.

QUIZ No. 42

In the next set of examples the climate is less favourable for intervention since (*a*) you are vulnerable and opponents are not; (*b*) the player on your left has opened the bidding and has heard his partner's response and will be quick to double if you run into his second suit; and (*c*) your partner has not overcalled at the level of One, so cannot be strong.

East–West are vulnerable and the bidding has gone:

South	West	North	East
1 ♣	No	1 ♥	?

What should East bid on the following hands?

(162) ♠ A 7   ♥ 6 2   ♦ K Q J 7 4 3   ♣ 8 4 2

(163) ♠ K J 7 4 2   ♥ A Q 9 4   ♦ J 4 2   ♣ 5

(164) ♠ Q 10 9 8 7 4   ♥ 5 3   ♦ 4   ♣ A J 8 5

ANSWERS TO QUIZ No. 42

(162) Two Diamonds. You might run into a penalty of 800, it is true, but you are showing a good lead against no-trumps and by bidding at this level you prevent the opener from rebidding One Spade, 1 NT, or Two Clubs.

(163) No Bid. With the strong hearts and singleton in clubs (which partner may hold) you have better defensive than offensive prospects.

(164) One Spade. You are weak in high cards but you can risk bidding at the One level because the spades are solid apart from the top cards. One advantage of the bid is that should South become declarer at no-trumps you head partner away from an unattractive diamond lead.

Defensive Overcalls

Responding to Partner's Overcall

Partnership bidding in defence is conducted on a more down-to-earth basis than by the side that has opened the bidding. A simple change of suit is not forcing and partner's suit should be supported when possible. Less trump support is required than when raising an opening bid. That is especially so when partner has overcalled at the level of Two and is marked with a good suit.

Quiz No. 43

Neither side is vulnerable and the bidding goes:

South	West	North	East
1 ♦	1 ♠	No	?

What should East bid on the following hands?

(165)   ♠ 8 4 3   ♥ A 8 3   ♦ K 9 7 6   ♣ K 10 4

(166)   ♠ J 7 4   ♥ 5   ♦ 7 4 3 2   ♣ A 9 7 6 4

(167)   ♠ Q 8 6   ♥ Q 4 3 2   ♦ 6   ♣ A K 8 5 3

Answers to Quiz No. 43

(165) 1 NT. In responding to an overcall at the level of One, the limits for 1 NT are from about 8 to 11 points.

(166) Two Spades. Game is unlikely but it may well be a good tactical move to raise the level of the bidding before South (who probably has a strong hand) can speak again.

(167) Three Spades. You have the values and Two Clubs, remember, would not be forcing.

Quiz No. 44

Both sides are vulnerable and the bidding has gone:

South	West	North	East
1 ♠	2 ♥	No	?

What should East bid on the following hands?

(168)   ♠ Q J 4   ♥ Q 3   ♦ A 8 3   ♣ J 8 7 4 2

(169)   ♠ 8 4   ♥ 7 5 2   ♦ A K J 4   ♣ A 9 5 3

(170)   ♠ Q 6 2   ♥ 6   ♦ 10 7 4   ♣ K J 8 5 3 2

More About Bidding

(168) 2 NT. Partner has overcalled at the level of Two, vulnerable, and must be quite strong. You have enough to raise the hearts but your holding in spades suggests a no-trump contract.

(169) Four Hearts. It is uncommon to give a double raise on three small trumps, but partner must have a good suit, the more so as you have these top cards in the minors.

(170) No Bid. In general it is bad to make what are known as 'rescue' bids. You may not care for Two Hearts but you have no reason to suppose that your clubs are better than partner's hearts. Even if Two Hearts were doubled it would be a mistake to rescue.

Jump Overcalls

A jump overcall, such as Two Spades over One Club, or Three Diamonds over One Heart, is strong but not forcing. The value in terms of high cards is likely to be from about 12 to 16.

The player on your right having opened One Diamond, you would overcall Two Hearts on either of the following hands:

1. ♠ 4   ♥ A Q J 9 7 6   ♦ A 4   ♣ K J 5 3

2. ♠ 7 4   ♥ A K Q J 6   ♦ 8 6 5 2   ♣ A Q

Overcalls of 1 NT

When an opponent has opened the bidding an overcall of 1 NT shows in principle the same strength as an original 1 NT—that is to say, 16 to 18 points.

Neither side is vulnerable and the opponent on your right opens One Heart. You hold:

1. ♠ K 6   ♥ K J 4   ♦ J 7 3   ♣ A Q J 10 4

With your double guard in hearts and good clubs you can well shade by one point and overcall 1 NT.

2. ♠ A J 5   ♥ K 9 7   ♦ K Q 10 8   ♣ K Q 6

This is a typical hand for the overcall of 1 NT.

3. ♠ Q J 4   ♥ K J 10 8 3   ♦ A 5   ♣ K Q 4

Defensive Overcalls

It would not be a bad mistake to overcall 1 NT on this hand, but with so much strength in the enemy suit the usual manœuvre is to make what is known as a 'trap pass'. That would certainly be the best plan if the opponents were vulnerable.

Overcalls in the Protective Position

So far in this chapter we have been considering 'immediate' overcalls: that is, overcalls of the bid made on the player's right. Rather different in kind are defensive calls when there have been two passes, as in the following sequences:

	South	*West*	*North*	*East*
1.	1 ♥	No	No	?
2.	1 ♥	No	2 ♥	No
	No	?		

East in example (1) is said to be in the 'protective' position. It is not a very good description, but it means that East is in a position where he may have to protect his partner's pass, it being assumed that partner may have made a trap pass.

The requirements for a bid in this position are lower than for immediate overcalls, partly because there is generally an inference that partner has a good hand, and partly because a player who overcalls in this position is not so much exposed to a penalty double. Thus after One Heart has been followed by two passes East holds:

♠ A J 8 7　♥ 6 4　♦ K 10 6 3　♣ Q 4 3

It is quite in order to re-open the bidding with One Spade. Inexperienced players are liable to reflect only that opponents will not go far in One Heart. That is true, but part scores have considerable value and the difference between making a part score yourself and letting the opponents make one is between two and three hundred, for you will realize that a part score, like a game, has a value beyond what appears on the score-sheet.

Now take the second sequence mentioned above:

More About Bidding

South	West	North	East
1 ♥	No	2 ♥	No
No	?		

It is game all and West holds:

♠ K 10 6 4 2 ♥ 7 4 2 ♦ A Q 3 ♣ 4 2

It was right not to make a vulnerable overcall of One Spade on the first round, but strangely enough it is not at all dangerous to bid Two Spades now. You can take the following points into consideration:

1. Since opponents have stopped in Two Hearts they presumably lack game values. That means that they are unlikely to have more than 23 points between them in top cards and quite possibly have less. As there are 40 points in the pack and you have only 9, partner must have 8 and may well have more.

2. Since North's response to One Heart was a limited raise to Two, it is most unlikely that he will have a hand on which he can double Two Spades.

3. Hearts have been bid and supported and you have three of them. It is therefore likely that partner has a doubleton or singleton, and consequently there is a fair chance both that he will have some spades with you and that the two hands will fit well.

Arguments of this sort are perhaps a little advanced for players learning the game, but the fact is that judgment in challenging for part scores is a very important factor in successful play. That is why we have set out to start you thinking along the right lines.

Quiz No. 45

Both sides are vulnerable and the bidding has gone:

South	West	North	East
1 ♦	No	No	?

What should East bid on the following hands:

(171) ♠ A J 4 ♥ Q J 8 ♦ K 10 7 ♣ Q 9 6 2

(172) ♠ K Q 10 8 6 3 ♥ A 4 ♦ 7 2 ♣ Q 5 3

(173) ♠ Q 4 ♥ K 9 6 3 ♦ K J 10 8 ♣ A J 7

(174) ♠ J 10 4 ♥ K 9 8 6 3 ♦ 4 ♣ A 8 4 2

Defensive Overcalls

(171) 1 NT. This is not a strong bid in the protective position. The limits are from about 12 to 14.

(172) Two Spades. To show that you are re-opening on a very fair hand with a good suit.

(173) No Bid. With this strength in the opponent's suit your best plan is to try to defeat One Diamond. If by any chance 3 NT is on for you, the loss will not be great, for you will score 300 or so defending against One Diamond.

(174) One Heart. The fact that you are short in diamonds makes it more likely that partner has made a trap pass. Do not be too much afraid that opponents will come to life and bid to game in spades. That will happen very rarely.

15

Take-out Doubles

There is one very useful call so familiar to bridge players that they scarcely think of it as a convention at all. This is the so-called 'take-out double'. Its effect is that a double of a suit call at a low level does not signify intention to defeat the contract but asks partner to name his best suit. To give the commonest example, the opponent on your right opens One Diamond and you hold:

♠ K J 7 3　♥ A 10 8 5　♦ 4　♣ K Q 6 2

If you double, that means that you have a useful hand yourself and want to know where your partner's strength lies.

It is naturally very important to distinguish between a normal penalty double and a take-out double. The following definition holds good for almost all situations:

If partner has already made a bid of any kind, then a double is a penalty double made with the expectation of defeating the contract.

If partner has not made a bid, a double of One or Two in a suit is for a take-out if made at the first opportunity of doubling.

The logic of the situation is that when partner has already shown where his strength lies there is no point in doubling for a take-out.

Quiz No. 46

In the following bidding sequences, are the doubles for penalties or for a take-out?

132

Take-out Doubles

	South	West	North	East
(175)	1 ♥	No	2 ♥	Double
(176)	1 ♠	Double(a)	2 ♣	Double(b)
(177)	1 ♠	No	1 NT	No
	2 ♠	Double		
(178)	1 ♥	Double(a)	2 ♥	No
	No	Double(b)		
(179)	1 ♦	1 ♥	No	2 ♥
	Double			

ANSWERS TO QUIZ No. 46

(175) For a take-out: partner has not made a bid.

(176) (*a*) For a take-out.
     (*b*) For penalties, as partner has made a call other than a pass.

(177) For penalties, as West did not double spades at the first opportunity. (If good enough to double Two Spades for a take-out, obviously he would have doubled One Spade.)

(178) (*a*) For a take-out.
     (*b*) For a take-out. West is still trying to stir his partner to action.

(179) For a take-out. It is quite common for the side that has opened the bidding to double for a take-out.

The Doubler's Requirements

The requirements for a double vary according to circumstances. To double an opening bid on your right you should have upwards of 11 points together with good distribution. Good distribution in this case means that you must be prepared for any response that partner may make.

In the following examples neither side is vulnerable and the player on your right has opened One Diamond. You hold:

1. ♠ A J 6 4   ♥ K 10 7 5 3   ♦ 2   ♣ K J 4

This is excellent distribution for a double, especially as you have length in both majors.

2. ♠ 4 2   ♥ K 10 9 6 4   ♦ A 7 3   ♣ K Q 4

Now your distribution is not so strong and you would be in a poor contract if partner had to respond in spades on a four-card suit. You should make a simple overcall of One Heart.

3. ♠ A 4   ♥ A K J 8 5 3   ♦ 4 2   ♣ K Q 4

You have a good enough suit now for a jump overcall, but with 17 points in high cards you should begin by doubling. Then you bid your hearts on the next round.

QUIZ No. 47

At game all South opens One Heart. What should West call on the following hands?

(180)   ♠ A 3   ♥ K J 10 5   ♦ K 9 6 5   ♣ Q J 4

(181)   ♠ Q 10 8 6   ♥ —   ♦ A J 10 6 4   ♣ K 9 6 2

(182)   ♠ K 9 2   ♥ A Q 8   ♦ A J 10 5   ♣ K Q 10

(183)   ♠ 7 6 4   ♥ A 8 3   ♦ A K 5 2   ♣ K 7 6

ANSWERS TO QUIZ No. 47

(180) No Bid. With so much strength in the enemy suit a trap pass is preferable to a double. The opponents may well be headed for a penalty.

(181) Double. The strong support for any suit that partner may call compensates for the moderate holding in high cards.

(182) Double. With 19 points and two 10's you are strong for 1 NT. You double and bid no-trumps on the next round.

(183) No Bid. This is not a trap pass, but the hand is unsuited for offensive action. You may have a chance to enter the auction later.

Responding to Take-out Doubles

Say that the bidding has begun in the following manner:

South	West	North	East
1 ♥	Double	No	?

Take-out Doubles

East, the partner of the player who has made a take-out double, now acts according to the following principles:

1. With a weak or moderate hand he makes a minimum response in his best suit or, with a guard in the enemy suit, bids 1 NT.

2. With a fair hand, about 8 to 10 points, he makes a jump response in the suit or bids 2 NT.

3. With exceptional strength in the opponent's suit he may pass, converting the take-out double into a penalty double.

4. To show a certain game hand, in conjunction with partner's double, he bids the opponent's suit.

Quiz No. 48

At love all the bidding goes:

South	West	North	East
1 ♥	Double	No	?

What should East bid on the following hands?

(184) ♠ 8 4   ♥ 6 3 2   ♦ J 5 4 3   ♣ 9 6 4 2

(185) ♠ Q 10 6 4   ♥ 9 8 5   ♦ A 7 4 2   ♣ K 3

(186) ♠ J 4   ♥ K 10 8 6 3   ♦ 7 4 3 2   ♣ 9 5

(187) ♠ A 10 6 5   ♥ 10 7   ♦ A Q 6 2   ♣ Q J 4

(188) ♠ 7   ♥ Q J 10 8 7 6   ♦ Q 10 5   ♣ 7 4 2

Answers to Quiz No. 48

(184) Two Clubs. An unhappy situation, but to pass would be a bad mistake. (It would be different if North had made a bid: then East would not be required to speak on a bad hand.)

(185) Two Spades. Quite a good hand in response to a double. Remember that partner is likely to be short of hearts, so the losers in that suit are not necessarily a weakness.

(186) 1 NT. The hearts are not strong enough for a penalty pass.

(187) Two Hearts, the way to show that you see a certain game. Rather than plunge into Four Spades, which might be a mistake, you ask partner to describe his hand.

More About Bidding

(188) No Bid. This is the only sort of hand on which a penalty pass is advisable when sitting under the opponent. Note that your hearts are so strong that you would welcome a heart lead so that you could draw the declarer's trumps.

Action by the Opener's Partner

We turn now to the partner of the player whose opening bid has been doubled. The bidding has begun:

South	West	North	East
1 ♠	Double	?	

North acts as follows:

1. With a fair to moderate hand he bids naturally.

2. With a poor hand but support for partner's suit, he raises to the limit.

3. With a strong hand, either defensively or in support of partner, he redoubles.

These are some examples, the bidding having gone as above at game all:

1. ♠ 10 7   ♥ J 4 2   ♦ 8 3   ♣ K Q 10 7 5 4

Bid Two Clubs. Because of the failure to redouble, the bid is limited in strength and not forcing.

2. ♠ 8 4   ♥ Q J 9 3   ♦ A 10 8 6 2   ♣ K 4

Redouble. It is quite likely that you will catch the vulnerable opponents for a penalty. You can deal with either red suit and partner, knowing that you have about 10 points or more, may be able to double Two Clubs.

3. ♠ Q J 8 5   ♥ 6 2   ♦ K 10 7 6 2   ♣ 6 3

Jump to Three Spades. Partner will know that you are bidding defensively, for with the values for a normal Three Spades, including some high cards, you would first redouble.

Other Doubling Situations

We have been studying mainly doubles of an opening bid by second hand, but there are many other uses of the take-out double which we can review briefly.

136

Take-out Doubles

Doubling after a pass

A player who has already passed has licence to double on as little as 9 or 10 points when he has especially good distribution.

At game to East–West the bidding goes:

South	West	North	East
No	1 ♦	No	1 ♥
?			

South holds:

♠ Q J 9 4   ♥ 3   ♦ 6 4 2   ♣ A Q 10 6 3

Having passed originally, he can double now to show that he sees possibilities of defence in either black suit.

Double by a player who has opened

A player who has opened the bidding and has reserves of strength may double later in an attempt to extract some life from his partner. Thus the bidding goes:

South	West	North	East
1 ♦	1 ♠	No	No

South holds:

♠ 3   ♥ A J 9 4   ♦ A Q J 9 5   ♣ K Q 10

South doubles now, for that gives his partner much wider choice of action than would a rebid of Two Hearts. Over the double partner may bid hearts himself, or return to diamonds, or bid clubs or no-trumps. Finally, he may have strength in spades and pass the double, playing to defeat One Spade doubled. If that happened, any further doubles by either player would be for penalties. Thus, suppose the bidding to continue:

South	West	North	East
1 ♦	1 ♠	No	No
Double	No	No	2 ♥
Double			

This second double by South would be for penalties. North has not made a bid in the legal sense, but his penalty pass of One Spade doubled was an indication that his best suit was spades.

More About Bidding

Double in the protective position

Like overcalls in the protective position (see page 129), doubles can be somewhat shaded. The bidding goes:

South	West	North	East
1 ♥	No	No	?

East holds:

♠ Q J 4   ♥ 7 5   ♦ K J 8 5   ♣ A 6 4 2

East can re-open with a double. That will suit West particularly well if his main strength is in hearts.

Double of 1 NT

You may recall that the definition of take-out doubles confined them to doubles of a suit call at the level of One or Two. It is impractical to double 1 NT for a take-out, the main reason being that the doubler cannot have length in all four suits and partner will often take out into the weakest suit.

In principle, doubles of 1 NT are for penalties. The doubler should be at least as strong as the no-trump opener or should have a suit which he can safely call in the event of trouble.

South opens 1 NT and as West you hold:

1. ♠ Q 7 4   ♥ A J 8 4   ♦ J 7 6   ♣ A K 5

It is too dangerous to double. There is at least as good a hand as yours on your right and if the balance is held by North he will redouble and your side may be caught for a big penalty. (You would be entitled to double 1 NT if your opponents were playing a weak no-trump of 13 to 15 points.)

2. ♠ K Q J 9 6 4   ♥ A Q 5   ♦ K 5 3   ♣ 4

Now you are better placed to double, for if partner passes you can set up your spades right away, and if partner rescues into Two Clubs you will not come to great harm in Two Spades.

The doubler's partner should generally pass on a balanced hand, even if weak.

Take-out Doubles

♠ 10 6 4 2 ♥ J 7 6 3 ♦ J 6 2 ♣ 4 3

Pass a double of 1 NT rather than try to make a contract at the Two level.

♠ J 7 5 2 ♥ J 8 4 2 ♦ 3 ♣ 7 5 4 2

Now take out the double into Two Clubs, the lowest ranking suit, and hope eventually to land on your feet.

S.O.S. redouble

There are a few situations in which a redouble at a low level asks for a rescue. The bidding goes:

South	West	North	East
1 ♣	Double	No	No
Redouble			

If South were happy about playing in One Club doubled he would pass. Having bid One Club on a short suit perhaps, he redoubles to induce his partner to try some other suit.

This is not a technique that we recommend you to try out with a learner sitting opposite, but we mention it lest you have a fierce encounter with a partner who will expect you to know what his redouble signifies.

16

Some Special Situations

One type of call that we have not discussed (except as a response to a take-out double) is a bid of the opponent's suit. Sometimes this means a genuine holding, but much more often it is a conventional way of forcing to game.

A Bid of the Opponent's Suit

It will happen sometimes that an opponent will open One Heart, say, and sitting over him you will have a very strong holding such as A Q 10 8 7 6. You must not overcall Two Hearts, for that would have an entirely different meaning. For the moment you can either pass or, with a strong hand outside as well, double. When you bid the opponent's suit later, it will be assumed that you want to play in that suit. Thus in both the following sequences West makes a genuine call in the enemy suit:

	South	West	North	East
1.	1 ♦	No	1 NT	No
	No	2 ♦		
2.	1 ♦	Double	No	1 ♥
	No	2 ♦		

As an immediate overcall

Apart from sequences like the above, a bid of the opponent's suit is an artificial way of showing great strength. One important use is as an overcall on exceptionally powerful hands. Thus South opens One Heart and West holds:

140

Some Special Situations

1. ♠ K Q J 4   ♥ —   ♦ A K 10 8 7   ♣ A Q J 3

Here Two Hearts is used as a kind of super-double. The bid is traditionally played as forcing to game, but the modern tendency is to allow the strong hand to stop short on occasions.

2. ♠ A Q 8 6 4   ♥ 3   ♦ A K 10 8 7 6   ♣ A

The forcing overcall is indispensable on this kind of two-suiter. Partner responds to this forcing overcall in the same way as to a take-out double, naming his best suit.

As a subsequent force

At any time later in the bidding the call of an opponent's suit can be used to ensure that game be reached. Here it is used by the defending side:

South	West	North	East
1 ♦	1 ♥	No	?

East holds:

1. ♠ A J 4   ♥ K J 10 5   ♦ 4   ♣ A K J 5 3

A simple raise to Four Hearts would be unenterprising and a jump to Six Hearts precipitous. East should bid Two Diamonds, forcing to game, so that he can explore slam possibilities at leisure.

2. ♠ A K 8 7   ♥ Q 3   ♦ A 8 2   ♣ K Q 4 2

Now East cannot be sure what the contract will be, but for the moment he must signal to partner, by calling Two Diamonds, that game appears certain.

When used by the attacking side the bid in most cases confirms strong support for partner's suit. The bidding begins:

South	West	North	East
1 ♥	No	1 ♠	2 ♣
2 ♣			

South's Three Clubs is forcing to game, is almost surely based on strong support for spades, and usually, though not necessarily, betokens first-round control (Ace or void) of clubs.

141

More About Bidding

Neither side is vulnerable and the bidding goes:

South	West	North	East
1 ♥	1 ♠	?	

What should North bid on the following hands?

(189)   ♠ A K 4   ♥ Q 7   ♦ Q 7 4 2   ♣ A K 8 6

(190)   ♠ 6   ♥ A Q 10 5   ♦ K J 7 6   ♣ A 6 4 2

(191)   ♠ —   ♥ Q 9 6 2   ♦ K J 8 6 4   ♣ Q 10 4 3

(192)   ♠ A 4   ♥ K 10 7   ♦ A Q J 8 5 4   ♣ K 2

ANSWERS TO QUIZ No. 49

(189) Three Clubs. To bid Two Spades would appear to confirm hearts as the trump suit and would make it almost impossible to find what might be a better contract in a minor suit or possibly in no-trumps.

(190) Two Spades. Not necessarily a slam hand opposite One Heart, but too strong for a simple jump to Four Hearts. The hand is expressed by the overcall in spades followed by support to Four Hearts.

(191) Four Hearts. The fact that you are void of spades does not mean that you have to use the forcing overcall. The raise to game is both tactically superior and a better expression of values.

(192) Three Diamonds. Two Spades would not be a mistake, but it is better to show the diamond suit. If partner rebids Three Hearts, then you can bid Three Spades.

Defence to Pre-emptive Openings

All experienced players have some special system of defence against an opponent's pre-emptive opening. We suggest that you use the following method:

When an opponent has opened Three of a minor, use a double as a request for a take-out, 3 NT as natural.

Some Special Situations

When an opponent has opened Three of a major, double for penalties and bid 3 NT for a take-out.

In the protective position (3 ♥—No—No—Double) a double is always primarily for a take-out.

To use the take-out double over Three of a minor you should be at least a Queen better than for a minimum double at the range of One. Bidding 3 NT over a major for a take-out is more hazardous because partner has to respond at the level of Four and is much more exposed to a double. You should be not less than an Ace stronger than for a double at the low range. (Remember that the minimum standard for a double of One is 11 points with good distribution such as 5—4—3—1, 13 points with fair distribution such as 4—4—3—2.)

QUIZ No. 50

Both sides are vulnerable and South opens Three Diamonds. What should West bid on the following hands?

(193)   ♠ A J 4   ♥ Q 8 6 3 2   ♦ 6 4   ♣ K J 7

(194)   ♠ A 4 3   ♥ J 4 2   ♦ K 6   ♣ A K Q 10 8

(195).   ♠ 7   ♥ A Q J 9 7 3   ♦ A 8   ♣ K Q J 2

ANSWERS TO QUIZ No. 50

(193) No Bid. Neither Three Hearts nor double would be at all safe. With a spade more and a diamond less you would double for a take-out.

(194) 3 NT. Not a certainty, but one has to take some risks against an opening pre-emptive call. If diamonds are led you have seven likely tricks in your own hand.

(195) Four Hearts. It would be a mistake to double, because partner might inconveniently jump in spades. Three Hearts would place too great a strain on partner: you want very little from him to make game.

QUIZ No. 51

Both sides are vulnerable and the bidding goes:

South	West	North	East
3 ♥	3 NT	No	?

More About Bidding

Bearing in mind that 3 NT over a major is equivalent to a strong take-out double, what should East bid on the following hands?

(196) ♠ 7 4 3 ♥ K 5 2 ♦ K 8 6 4 ♣ 9 4 2

(197) ♠ K Q 10 7 6 ♥ 6 4 3 ♦ 7 4 ♣ A 4 3

(198) ♠ Q 6 ♥ Q J 9 4 ♦ 6 3 ♣ J 7 6 4 2

ANSWERS TO QUIZ No. 51

(196) Four Diamonds. It would not be safe to pass 3 NT, for remember that the lead will come through your King of hearts.

(197) Five Spades. You would have had to bid Four Spades without the King of spades and the Ace of clubs, so you must certainly suggest a slam.

(198) No Bid. You hold the hearts strongly enough and 3 NT should be the best chance for game.

Defence against Four Bids

Over an opening bid of Four, 4 NT is always for a take-out and must clearly be strong—at least 16 points and good support for all three suits.

A double is primarily for penalties but should have a backing of high cards as well as tricks in the trump suit. Partner may take out if he has a good suit of his own.

Bidding from a Part Score

Possession of a part score makes no great difference to opening bids, except that the range of an opening 1 NT is extended for tactical reasons. With a score of 60 or more you can open 1 NT on anything from 14 to 20. This is always a difficult bid for opponents to combat because they have to defend at the level of Two and are very much exposed to a penalty double.

When a bid of Two Diamonds or Two Hearts or Two Spades will give you game you can reduce the normal requirements by at least a King or so. Thus at 40 up you hold:

♠ A Q J 10 7 6 ♥ 5 2 ♦ A K 10 3 ♣ 6

Some Special Situations

It is sound tactics to open Two Spades. If partner makes any response that takes the bidding above the game level you make a minimum rebid in your suit and that warns him that you were not up to normal strength for a Two bid.

Other opening bids have their normal significance. An opening Three bid, even when it carries you beyond game, is in principle pre-emptive, and Two Clubs is a conventional force as always.

Responding at a part score

Presence of a part score does not affect the normal forcing responses. Thus if partner opens One Diamond at 40 up and you respond Two Spades that is unconditionally forcing. If the opener is weak he will rebid diamonds or bid 2 NT.

When partner opens with a bid of One that is still short of game it is reasonable to lower the requirements for a minimum response by 2 points or so, but not more.

QUIZ No. 52

Both sides are vulnerable and North–South have a part score of 60. The bidding begins:

South	West	North	East
1 ♥	No	?	

How should North respond on the following hands?

(199) ♠ A 4 ♥ K 10 7 3 ♦ K 10 8 5 ♣ Q J 4

(200) ♠ J 8 7 5 2 ♥ 4 ♦ Q 7 4 2 ♣ 9 4 3

(201) ♠ Q 3 ♥ A J 5 ♦ K Q 6 3 ♣ A K 9 4

(202) ♠ K Q J 9 4 3 ♥ 4 2 ♦ J 8 7 4 ♣ 3

ANSWERS TO QUIZ No. 52

(199) Three Hearts. This takes you one over score but Three Hearts should be safe and is only a mild slam suggestion.

(200) No Bid. Occasionally you will find that you could have snatched game in Two Spades or some such contract, but more often, if you respond, you will end up by conceding a penalty or doubling opponents into game.

(201) Three Clubs, the normal force. If partner rebids Three Hearts you will give him one more chance by raising to Four Hearts.

(202) One Spade. You would like to jump to Two Spades, but that would have a different meaning. With seven spades instead of six you might jump to Three Spades: that would be pre-emptive, not a force.

The Approach to Slam

In view of the amount that is written about slam bidding in bridge books and articles, you may wonder why we deal with this subject so briefly and so late. The reason is that slam bidding is not a separate part of the game but an extension of earlier bidding.

Mathematics of slam bidding

The first thing you should know is the value of a slam as compared with game. If you go one down in a small slam, not vulnerable, you lose only 50 on the score-sheet, but your real loss, taking into account the game you have missed, is about 500. Since that is also the slam bonus it follows that you can bid a small slam on an even chance. The same is true when you are vulnerable.

To forgo a small slam by trying for a grand slam is more serious. You need odds of over 2 to 1 in favour. That means that it is unwise to bid a grand slam unless you can more or less count the tricks.

Slam tests

The easiest slams to judge are those when you have such weight in high cards that twelve tricks must be possible in some contract. If you can count 33 points in honour cards, then there should be a play for a slam even without the aid of a long suit. To take a simple example, suppose that partner were to open 1 NT and you had 17 points: then you would know that you had a minimum of 33 and were in the slam zone.

These are two tests that you can apply for slams in a suit:

Some Special Situations

1. *A slam is likely when the two hands contain between them the value for an opening bid on one side, plus the value for a jump rebid on the other.*

Example: partner opens One Heart and holding

♠ A 10 8 6 4   ♥ Q 3   ♦ A Q 4   ♣ 6 3 2

you respond One Spade. Partner jumps to Three Hearts. Now you have the values for an opening bid, including two Aces, plus a valuable bolster in hearts. You could go straight to Six Hearts. Don't worry about the losing clubs: it is strong odds on partner having a control.

2. *A slam is at any rate worth exploring if you judge that you could take an Ace away from your hand and still be confident of game.*

Example: partner opens One Diamond and holding

♠ K Q 6 5 2   ♥ 8 3   ♦ Q J 2   ♣ A J 6

you respond One Spade. Partner raises to Three Spades. Now you could certainly reckon to make game with an Ace less than you hold, and your values include fair trumps and the Q J of your partner's suit. A slam should be on if the hands fit well —but there could be two losers in hearts. In fact you should make what is known as a cue bid of Four Clubs, indicating a control in that suit and inviting a slam. That is a new concept and brings us on to the next section.

Cue bids

When a suit has been strongly supported, as by a double raise, a bid of a new suit at the Four level is a cue bid. Take the sequence just described:

West	East
1 ♦	1 ♠
3 ♠	4 ♣

Four Clubs is a cue bid, one of North's objects being to discover whether partner controls the hearts. Suppose that the two hands are as follows:

West	East
♠ A 10 8 4	♠ K Q 6 5 2
♥ A 10 4	♥ 8 3
♦ A K 7 3	♦ Q J 2
♣ 8 2	♣ A 6 4

Over Four Clubs West (having already bid diamonds) will make a cue bid of Four Hearts. East will then go to Six Spades.

Blackwood

There are also ways of showing a number of Aces in a single bid. The most popular of these is the Blackwood convention. In this convention 4 NT asks partner to state how many Aces he holds. Partner responds according to the following pattern:

With no Ace or four Aces	Five Clubs
With one Ace	Five Diamonds
With two Aces	Five Hearts
With three Aces	Five Spades

If the player who bid 4 NT follows with 5 NT, then responder shows how many Kings he has according to the same schedule.

This convention has a deceptive simplicity and is over-used by the majority of players. The fact is that most slams depend not solely on Aces but on a variety of assets such as an extra trump, an odd Queen, a well-placed singleton, and so on. We think that you should understand Blackwood and humour a partner who employs it, but we advise you to use the convention yourself only on rare hands when you are interested in nothing but Aces.

Glossary of Bridge Terms and Phrases*

Above the Line. The line is the line on the score-sheet. All scores except those for tricks bid and made (such as 60 for Two Spades) are entered above this line.

Auction. The bidding, the period during which it takes place.

Balanced. A hand with balanced distribution is one containing no short suits. Most balanced is 4-3-3-3, then 5-3-3-2 and 4-4-3-2.

Below the Line. Scores for tricks bid and made (such as 100 when 3 NT is bid and nine or more tricks made) are entered below the line on the score-sheet.

Bid. When a player makes a bid he undertakes to win a specified number of tricks either with no-trumps or with a specified suit as trumps. According to the definition of the Laws, neither a pass nor a double or redouble is technically a bid.

Biddable Suit. A suit normally considered strong enough to be named as a natural bid.

Bidding. The period from the first call, after the deal has been completed, up to the final pass.

Blackwood. The name (after its founder) of a popular convention whereby partner is asked to indicate, by means of a conventional response, the number of Aces (and sometimes Kings) that he holds.

Book. The book is an old-fashioned term for the first six tricks made by the declarer.

---

* This glossary is confined to terms arising from this book —T.R.

Glossary of Bridge Terms and Phrases

Call. A comprehensive term which includes a pass, double or re-double, as well as a bid.

Cash. When a player has a winning card that he can play off whenever he wants to, he is said to cash the trick.

Clear a Suit. Either declarer or a defender can clear a suit for his side by driving out adverse winners so that he or his partner will win the rest of the tricks.

Combination. A combination finesse is one taken when two adjacent high cards are missing, as when declarer holds A J 10 and misses K Q.

Competitive. Bidding is competitive when both sides enter the auction.

Contract. The final contract is that named by the final bid of the auction. The contract may be undoubled, doubled, or re-doubled. 'Four Hearts' means Four Hearts undoubled and is a contract to win ten tricks with hearts as trumps.

Control. When a player has the Ace of a suit he has first round control. A King or, in a suit contract, a singleton is second-round control. A declarer has trump control when he has enough trumps to draw those of his opponents and retain the lead.

Convention. When there is an agreement between partners that a bid or play should have a special meaning not obvious on the surface, that is a convention. The artificial opening of Two Clubs, unrelated to the club suit, is an example.

Cross-ruff. When declarer takes ruffs in the two hands alternately he plays a cross-ruff.

Cue bid. A bid that shows a control, such as Ace or King, rather than a normal biddable suit.

Cut. The draw for partners at the beginning of the game; the dividing of the pack into two parts when presented to the dealer.

Deal. The process of distributing cards one by one, thirteen to each player. Collectively, the four hands, their bidding and play.

Declarer. The player who first names the denomination, a suit or no-trumps, that wins the final contract is the declarer and in the play handles dummy's cards as well as his own.

150

Deep finesse. A finesse taken when there are two or more higher cards outstanding: for example, a finesse of the 9 from A Q 9.

Defender. During the bidding, the side whose opponents opened the bidding is the defending side. During the play, the opponents of the declarer are the defenders, their play the defence.

Denomination. The particular suit or no-trumps in which a contract is played.

Discard. A player who is unable to follow suit and plays a card of another suit (not the trump suit) makes a discard.

Distribution. The pattern of a player's hand, such as four cards of one suit, three of each of the others, is his distribution. Equally, each suit is distributed among the four players in a particular fashion.

Double. A double of an opponent's bid, if left in, increases the penalties should the contract not be made or increases the score for the opponents if they are successful.

Double finesse. A finesse that seeks to entrap two cards, as when the 10 is finessed from A Q 10.

Double raise. Support for partner's call that raises the bidding by two stages, as from One Spade to Three Spades.

Doubleton. A holding of two cards in a suit. K x is described as King doubleton.

Draw. To draw trumps, or draw any other suit, is to play out winning cards, extracting those held by the opponents.

Duck. When a player for tactical reasons plays a low card.

Dummy. The partner of the declarer; his hand, which is exposed on the table after the opening lead.

Entry. A winning card that affords entry to a player's hand.

Establish. A suit is established when the winning cards held by the opponents have been forced out.

Finesse. A player takes a finesse when he attempts to win or establish a trick by playing a card from the opposite hand that is not the highest held. Thus, when leading towards A Q, the play of the Queen is a finesse that will succeed if the King is favourably placed.

Fit. Two opposite hands are said to fit when their values do not

overlap; for example, when one player has A x x x of a side
suit and his partner a singleton together with sufficient trumps.

Follow suit. To play a card of the same suit as that led.

Force. In bidding, a call that obliges partner to respond, either
for one round or until game is reached, according to the nature
of the force. In play, a forcing lead is one that obliges an
opponent to use a trump if he wants to win the trick.

Free bid. A free bid, raise, rebid, or response, is one made after
an intervening call. Thus after One Heart by South, One
Spade by West, Two Hearts by North is a free raise.

Game. To score game, a side must score 100 for tricks below the
line. This can be done in one hand or by way of two or more
part scores.

Grand slam. A contract to win all thirteen tricks.

Hold-up. When for tactical reasons a player declines to part with
a winning card he is said to hold up.

Honour. An Ace, King, Queen, Jack or 10. A bonus is scored for
four or five honours of the trump suit all in one hand, or for
four Aces in one hand at no-trumps.

Insufficient bid. In law, a bid that is not sufficient to overcall the
previous bid.

Intermediates. Useful cards lower than a Jack, such as 10s, 9s
and 8s.

Intervening bid. A bid by the defending side. To bid without intervention means without opposition.

Jump. A jump bid, raise, rebid, response, or overcall, is a bid
higher—generally one range higher—than is required to overcall the preceding bid.

Lead. The first card played to a trick is the lead. The opening lead
is made by the defender on the left of the declarer. Thereafter
the winner of a trick leads to the next trick.

Limit. A limit bid is one that describes the strength of player's
hand within fairly narrow limits. Thus a single raise is a limit
bid because it cannot be strong.

Line. The horizontal line across the centre of the score-sheet;
scores in respect of tricks bid and made are entered below the
line, all others above the line.

Glossary of Bridge Terms and Phrases

Long cards. Low cards that become winners after a suit has been established are described as long cards.

Major suit. Spades and hearts are major suits. A contract at the level of Four from a love score produces game.

Minor suit. Diamonds and clubs are minor suits. A contract at the level of Five from a love score is required for game.

No Bid. Call expressing a desire to pass.

No-trumps. Denomination in which the suits are all equal in the play, there being no trump suit. A contract at the level of Three from a love score produces game.

Odd tricks. Tricks won by declarer beyond the number of six. To win the odd trick is to make seven tricks.

Open. To make the first bid; to make the opening lead.

Opener. The player who made the opening bid of the auction.

Overcall. A bid, generally by the defending side, that is of higher rank than the preceding bid.

Over-ruff. To play a trump higher than that with which another player has already ruffed.

Overtrick. A trick beyond the number for which declarer has contracted. Thus if the contract is Three Spades and declarer makes eleven tricks he has made two overtricks.

Part score. A score below the line of less than 100, not sufficient for game.

Pass. Call that a player makes at his turn when he does not wish to make a bid or to double or redouble; generally expressed by the words 'No bid'.

Penalty. Points scored above the line when an opponent has failed to make his contract.

Penalty double. A double whose object is to penalize the opponents, as opposed to a take-out double.

Penalty pass. When the partner of a player who has made a take-out double decides to pass for penalties, that is a penalty pass.

Peter. Method of signalling in defence to encourage partner to lead or continue a suit. The peter may consist of one high card or of two cards played in high-low order.

Point-count. An artificial method of valuation by assigning a point value to high cards and to certain distributional assets.

Glossary of Bridge Terms and Phrases

Positive response. A response to a conventional forcing bid, such as Two Clubs, that promises certain values.

Pre-emptive. A pre-emptive bid, opening, response, or overcall, is one made at a high level with the object of buying the contract or at least making communication difficult for the opponents.

Preference. When presented by partner with the choice of two suits, a player can give silent preference by passing the second suit, or can give simple or jump preference to the first suit.

Protective bid. One that is made in the last position, when the bidding would otherwise die, and based on the presumption that partner has undiscovered values. The simplest example is when an opening bid is followed by two passes.

Quitted trick. One that has been gathered and turned down. A quitted trick may be inspected until the player or his partner has led or played to the next trick.

Raise. Direct support for partner's call, as when One Heart is raised to Two Hearts.

Rank. No-trumps is the highest ranking call, followed by spades, hearts, diamonds, clubs. In the play cards rank in the order: Ace, King, Queen, Jack, 10 and so on down to the 2.

Rebid. The second bid made by any player is his rebid. The term usually refers to the opener's rebid.

Redouble. A call that can be made only when an opponent has doubled. If left in, it increases the penalties when the contract fails, and increases the trick score and bonus for overtricks when the contract succeeds.

Re-open. To make a bid or double in the last (protective) position when the bidding would otherwise have ended.

Responder. The player who responds to any specific call by his partner, such as the responder to a take-out double. When not otherwise defined, responder means the partner of the opening bidder.

Reverse. A player reverses when he bids at the level of Two a suit of higher rank than his first call. Thus a player who opens One Diamond and over a response of One Spade bids Two Hearts makes a reverse bid.

Glossary of Bridge Terms and Phrases

Revoke. A player who fails to follow suit when able to do so commits a revoke and is subject to penalty.

Rubber. When one side or the other has won two games, that is rubber. Scores are added and the present period of play is ended.

Ruff. To play a trump when a side suit has been led.

Sacrifice. A player makes a sacrifice bid when in order to save game or slam he makes a bid that he expects to be doubled and defeated.

Sequence. Three or more consecutive cards of a suit such as Q J 10. Q J 9 is a broken sequence, K 10 9 an inner sequence.

Side suit. In a trump contract, any suit other than the trump suit.

Sign-off. A bid that proclaims weakness and usually suggests that partner should pass.

Simple. A simple overcall, rebid, response, or take-out, is one made at a minimum level, as opposed to a jump.

Single raise. Support for partner's call that raises the bidding by only one stage, as when Two Clubs is raised to Three Clubs.

Singleton. A holding of one card of a suit.

Small slam. A contract to win twelve tricks.

S.O.S. redouble. A redouble that does not bear its normal meaning but asks partner to rescue.

Stopper. A card that arrests the run of enemy winners in a suit.

Take-out. A change of suit at a higher level, such as Two Diamonds over One Heart, a simple take-out.

Take-out double. A double that by convention asks partner to describe his hand, generally by bidding his best suit.

Top of nothing. The lead of the top card, generally from three low cards.

Trick. The play of four cards, one by each player, forms a trick.

Trump. Suit that in the play has superior rank to the others. This suit is determined by the bidding (except when there are no trumps), and is named in the final contract. To trump, to play a card of the trump suit when a side suit has been led (same as ruff).

Trump control. This belongs to the side that can cash its winners in the side suits after opposing trumps have been drawn.

155

Glossary of Bridge Terms and Phrases

Trump support. Sufficient holding in partner's suit to justify a raise.

Two-way finesse. Occurs when declarer can finesse against either player for a particular card, as when he has K 10 x opposite Q 9 x and can finesse against the Jack in either direction.

Unblock. To play or discard a card that might otherwise obstruct the run of a suit or win an unwelcome trick.

Undertrick. When a declarer fails to make his contract he fails by one or more undertricks.

Void. To be void of a suit is to have no cards of it.

Vulnerable. A side that has won a game becomes vulnerable, and thereafter penalties and some bonuses are increased.

Bidding Summary*

Valuation for high cards: 4 for Ace, 3 for King, 2 for Queen, 1 for Jack.

NO-TRUMP BIDS AND RESPONSES

When raising, add 1 point for a fair five-card suit.

Open 1 NT on 16 to 18. Raise to 2 NT on 7 to 8. Raise to 3 NT on 9. Simple take-out into Two of a suit not forcing.

Open 2 NT on 21 to 22. Raise to 3 NT on 4.

Open 3 NT with a solid minor suit and guards in two other suits.

OPENING SUIT BIDS

Add 2 points for a good six-card suit and in addition 1 point for each good five-card suit.

Open One of a suit with upwards of 13 points of which at least 11 are in high cards.

Open Two of a suit (other than clubs) with 19 to 22 points.

Open Two Clubs on near-game hands containing upwards of 23 points.

Open Three or Four of a suit on the basis of playing tricks, over-bidding by about three tricks when not vulnerable, two tricks when vulnerable.

---

* Do not be dismayed (still less write to the author) if the requirements in this summary do not exactly correspond with advice in the main text. That is partly because points for distribution were often not directly taken into account there, and partly because in a summary there is no space to record factors that might cause an adjustment—T.R.

Bidding Summary

When responding in a new suit add distributional points as for opening bids.

Respond 1 NT on 6 to 9, 2 NT on 11 to 13, 3 NT on 14 to 16.

Respond One of a suit on 6 to 15. This is forcing for one round.

Respond Two of a lower-ranking suit on 9 to 16. This is forcing for one round.

Jump in a new suit, forcing to game, with upwards of 16, or with less when holding exceptional support for partner.

Raise to Two with from 3 to 9 points according to trump support and ruffing values (i.e. short suits).

Raise to Three with from 5 to 12 points, according to trump support (usually four cards) and ruffing values.

Raise to Four with good trump support and 5 to 14 points, according to distribution.

REBIDS BY THE OPENER

Count distributional points as for opening bids except when there is evidence of a misfit.

(a) **After a response at the level of One**

Rebid 1 NT on 13 to 15, 2 NT on 16 to 18, 3 NT on 19 to 21.

Minimum rebid of suit or single raise: 13 to 15.

Simple change of suit: 13 to 18.

Reverse or jump rebid: 16 to 19.

Jump raise: with good trump support and 14 to 18 points, according to distribution.

Jump in a new suit, forcing to game: upwards of 19, or less when holding good support for partner.

(b) **After a simple response at the level of Two**

Rebid 2 NT on 15 to 17, 3 NT on 18 to 20.

Other rebids similar to those in (a), except that slightly less required for the stronger bids.

Bidding Summary

Count distributional points as for opening bids, except when there is evidence of a misfit.

(a) **When opener has made a limited rebid such as 1 NT, a repeat of his suit or a single raise**

With less than 10 points: generally pass on balanced hands.

With 10 to 12 points: make a constructive bid such as 2 NT or a change of suit or a jump rebid or a raise.

With upwards of 13 points: bid game or force by bidding a new suit at the range of Three.

(b) **When opener has made a simple bid in a new suit**

Over a rebid at the range of One:

Bid 1 NT on 7 to 10, 2 NT on 11 to 12.

Over a rebid at the range of Two:

Bid 2 NT on 9 to 11, 3 NT on 13, sometimes 12.

In general, when partner has changed the suit, pass only with a minimum 6 to 7 and no fit. With 7 to 9 make a minimum bid according to the nature of the hand, with 10 to 11 make a forward-going bid, and with 12 look for game.

DEFENSIVE OVERCALLS

A fair suit is assumed for an overcall, so do not count extra for distributional strength.

Simple overcalls range from 5 (non-vulnerable at the range of One) to 14.

Jump overcalls range from 12 to 16.

Take-out doubles range from 11 with strong distribution, or from 14 with fair distribution, up to near-game hands which are expressed by a forcing overcall in the opponent's suit.

Index

Scoring Table

Score below the line for tricks bid and made:

Spades or hearts	30 per trick	⎫ If doubled:
Diamonds or clubs	20 per trick	⎪ multiply by 2
No-trumps	40 for first trick	⎬ If redoubled:
	30 for each additional trick	⎭ multiply by 4

100 points wins game, but no separate score is recorded.

Score above the line:

	Overtricks	
	Not vulnerable	*Vulnerable*
Undoubled	Ordinary trick value	Ordinary trick value
Doubled	100 per trick	200 per trick
Redoubled	200 per trick	400 per trick

Making doubled or redoubled contract:

In addition to all other scores: 50.

Honours

4 trump honours in any one hand: 100.
5 trump honours in any one hand: 150.
4 Aces in one hand at no-trumps: 150.

Slams

	Not Vulnerable	*Vulnerable*
Small slam	500	750
Grand slam	1,000	1,500

161

Scoring Table

Penalties

	Not vulnerable	*Vulnerable*
Undoubled	50 each trick	100 each trick
Doubled	100 for first trick	200 for first trick
	200 for each additional trick	300 for each additional trick
Redoubled	Twice the above	Twice the above

Rubber Bonus

When the rubber is won in two games: 700.
When the rubber is won by two games to one: 500.

Unfinished Rubber

Bonus for a side that is game up: 300.
Bonus for a part score in an unfinished game: 50.